Books by Deborah Raney

A Vow to Cherish
In the Still of Night

A Vow TO Cherish

DEBORAH RANEY

BETHANY HOUSE PUBLISHERS
MINNEAPOLIS, MINNESOTA 55438

Published by Bethany House Publishers
A Ministry of Bethany Fellowship, Inc.
11300 Hampshire Avenue South
Minneapolis, Minnesota 55438

Printed in the United States of America.

Library of Congress Cataloging-in-Publication Data

Raney, Deborah.
    A vow to cherish / Deborah Raney.
        p.   cm.

    1. Alzheimer's disease—Patients—Family relationships—Fiction.
2. Married people—United States—Fiction. I. Title.
PS3568.A562V68   1996
813'.54—dc20   95-45105
ISBN 1–55661–666–X   CIP

To Daddy
and
To my husband, Ken

Two men whose integrity inspired
the character of Jake Brighton.

DEBORAH RANEY is a homemaker and first-time novelist. While busy raising four children, she is active in her local church and community in a variety of ways. She and her husband are the parents of three teenagers and a preschooler. They make their home in Kansas.

Acknowledgments

This novel would never have become a reality without the love, support, and encouragement of the following people:

Thank you, "Mothe," for reading to me when I was little, for instilling in me the love for libraries and literature that was the seed of this novel. Thank you to "Mothe" and Daddy and to my sisters for reading my manuscript in its earliest form and for encouraging me to keep writing.

Special thanks to Ellen Voth, Michelle DeHoogh-Kliewer, Doris DeHoogh, Tanya Keim, Kerry Grosch, Patrick Briar, and Claudia Luthi. Your suggestions and insights were invaluable to a beginning writer.

To my special friends, Marcy, Sharon, Terry, Lynn, and Mary—thank you for believing that I had a story to tell and for reminding me that I had a life apart from the computer! I love you guys.

Thank you, Sharon Madison and Ann Parrish at Bethany House, for your enthusiasm and encouragement. Your phone calls and letters kept me going.

DEBORAH RANEY

To Sharon Asmus, my editor, thank you for walking me through the process of writing this book, for making it such a hands-on experience. I learned so much from you, and I'm sure you were more patient than I'll ever know.

Most of all, thank you, Ken—for your support, your enthusiasm, your constant encouragement. Thank you for buying no-iron pants, ordering carry-out pizza, and taking Tavia to the park so I could keep writing. Thank you for being a man of God. I really, really couldn't have done it without you, honey.

And thank you, Lord, for the most priceless blessing of my life—my family: "Mothe" and Daddy, my grandparents, my brother, Brad, my sisters, Vicky and Beverly, and their families; Mom and Dad, Grandma and Grandpa, and all the rest of Ken's wonderful family; and for the most precious gifts of all—my husband, Ken, and our children, Tarl, Tobi, Trey, and Tavia. I have a rich heritage of love, and I am so very grateful.

Prologue

Jake rubbed his eyes, disoriented. He heard the drone of the shower in the bathroom and wondered why Ellen had allowed him to oversleep. Easing his long legs over the side of the bed, he tried to focus on the digital clock on his bedside table. The red numbers blurred and faded, but it looked like one-fifteen.

Not fully awake, he plodded into the bathroom. Through the steam of the shower he saw that Ellen's carriage clock on the counter read one-fifteen also.

"Ellen, what's wrong? Are you sick?"

"Well, sleepyhead," she called cheerfully through the curtain, "you're finally up. No, I'm not sick. What makes you ask that?"

"It's one o'clock in the morning, El. You just went to bed two hours ago."

"One o'clock? It can't be."

"Well it is." He yawned and sighed sleepily. "Come back to bed, you silly girl."

Wrapped in a thick white towel, she stepped from the

shower, her dark hair clinging in ringlets to her forehead and the nape of her neck in a way that Jake had always found appealing.

She leaned down and inspected the clock, disbelieving, then picked it up and held it to her ear, a confused laugh rising in her throat.

"That's strange . . . I could have sworn it was morning. Well, I feel pretty stupid."

She looked so bewildered that Jake thought for a minute she might truly be ill. But she dried off, retrieved her nightshirt from the floor, and followed her husband back to bed.

The next morning at breakfast Jake teased her about her nocturnal wandering, and they laughed together. Six months later he would look back to that incident as the inauspicious beginning of their nightmare.

1

The auditorium was crowded and stifling on an unseasonably warm May evening. The band tuned their instruments in hushed dissonance, and soon the strains of "Pomp and Circumstance" began to fill the air. Accompanied by the squeaking and grating of chairs, the audience rose to their feet and turned to watch the capped and gowned students file to the stage and mount the steps.

Kyle Brighton's family took up nearly one whole row of seats in the old auditorium. His grandparents, Howard and MaryEllen Randolph, sat in the center of this contingent. They were flanked by Kyle's sister, Jana, and her husband on one side, and Kyle's brother, Brant, on the other. Jake and Ellen Brighton sat at the end of the row, on the aisle, so they could snap a quick picture of their son as he marched to the front. Ellen spotted Kyle first and tugged on Jake's sleeve.

"Jake . . . Jake, what did you do with the camera?"

Jake looked on the seat behind him, then turned to Ellen, a puzzled look on his face. The camera had been there just moments before.

Ellen elbowed her husband and whispered excitedly, "Hurry, honey. He's almost here!"

Jake's eyes widened, and his shoulders shook with silent laughter as he pointed to the camera in Ellen's hand. She gave a little gasp and rolled her eyes in self-deprecation, shoving the camera in Jake's direction. He took it from her and quickly knelt in the aisle, waiting for the camera to focus. Kyle spotted his father and hammed a goofy grin just as the flash went off. Ellen shot Kyle an exaggerated scowl, and his smile turned genuine.

As the last crescendo peaked and receded, and the graduates took their seats on the dais, Jake reached for Ellen's hand. She turned and gave him a tight-lipped smile. They had been through this twice already, and Ellen thought she was immune to the emotional sentiment of the ceremony. But the music set off a rush of memories, and she found herself gulping back tears. She *couldn't* cry. Kyle would be mortified.

In truth, she wasn't being maudlin. She always cried on happy occasions, and she was jubilant that they had reached this milestone in their lives. Their last child had made his way safely through the labyrinth of adolescence, and this was undeniably a celebration of that fact. But Ellen always felt a bittersweetness about any transition in her life, and this one would certainly be significant.

In two weeks, Kyle would pack his bags and head to New Mexico for a summer job at a resort, and then in the fall he would start classes at the University of Illinois in Urbana. By the middle of June, 245 West Oaklawn would officially be an empty nest. While some of Ellen's friends had found the empty-nest stage a difficult passage, she was looking forward to it.

Perhaps some of her optimism was due to the fact that

her family still surrounded her. Jana and her husband lived nearby in Chicago and visited often. Brant was only two hours away at the university in Urbana. He wasn't quite as faithful about getting home, but they talked on the phone nearly every weekend.

It would be a comfort to Ellen to have the boys at school together. Kyle was going to be staying in the dorm for the first year at least, but Brant lived near the campus, and she knew he would keep an eye out for his little brother.

The commencement speaker stepped to the podium, and a hush descended over the auditorium. Ceremonies like this always brought a flood of memories to Ellen; it was as though her whole life passed before her. She felt so blessed by all that had brought her and Jake to this moment in their lives.

Ellen Randolph's childhood had been idyllic. Howard and MaryEllen Randolph worked their farm six days a week from sunup to sundown, and by the time their four daughters left home, the Randolphs owned their five hundred acres free and clear.

Having four daughters in succession had not disappointed Howard Randolph in the least, but neither had he made any concessions to their femininity. His girls could drive any tractor or truck on the place, and the miles of fence that surrounded their land had been mended by the Randolph sisters—Ellen, Kathy, Carol, and Diana. The Four Musketeers, their dad had called them—still called them.

The pleasures of Ellen's childhood on the Illinois farm came mostly from simple things—working side by side with her father in the fields, or gardening and canning in the steamy kitchen with her mother. Money was scarce, and though there had been occasional vacations—camping in the mountains or visiting relatives in California—these were not the substance of Ellen's memories. The magic lay in the everyday things: Sunday-night popcorn, catching fireflies behind the barn, snowball fights, and sledding till midnight on the frozen pond.

Her memories were full of grandmothers and grandfathers, aunts and uncles and cousins who seemed almost a part of her immediate family. She had a rich heritage of love and a legacy of faith that she had made her own at an early age.

Ellen graduated from college in her small hometown and six weeks later packed her bags and moved to Chicago, where she had accepted a position teaching kindergarten in North Lawndale, a rough inner-city neighborhood.

Ellen was a true farmer's daughter whose sole experience in the city up to that time had consisted of a field trip with her high school civics class. There, from the window of the chartered bus, she and a friend had witnessed a mugging in a dark alley of the Loop. They had shouted for the bus driver's attention and pleaded with him to stop and help, but no one else had actually seen it happen, and the driver dismissed it, saying, "Honey, these things happen every day in the city."

That incident made a deep impression on Ellen, and it defined Chicago for her the day her parents kissed her goodbye and left her alone in the city. Though she tried to act sophisticated and worldly-wise as she watched her parents' car disappear from sight, in truth she was scared to death.

Ellen had rented a small apartment, and though it was only eight blocks from the school, she took the bus to and from work. North Lawndale was not a safe place for a young woman to walk alone, even in the daytime. Ellen sometimes longed for the refuge of the farm, but she soon settled in to her teaching job, and it, at least, was a comfortable fit.

And then Jake Brighton came along.

From the time Ellen was a little girl wanting to marry her daddy, she'd had a romanticized picture of marriage. Howard and MaryEllen had always been openly affectionate, and the Randolph girls had a rosy paragon of marriage in their parents. But in her wildest dreams, Ellen couldn't have imagined how truly lovely being married would be, because Jake Brighton hadn't figured in her wildest dreams.

In the semidarkness of the auditorium, Ellen turned and looked up at her husband's strong profile. He seemed absorbed in the speaker's message, unmindful of her gaze. At fifty, his hair was graying at the temples, his eyes crinkled with lines, but he was still handsome, and Ellen often saw other women give him lingering glances. She was not jealous but proud that she could lay claim to this fascinating man. If anything riled her about Jake's handsomeness, it was the fact that men in general seemed to get more dignified looking as they aged, while women—herself included—had to fight the lines, the bulges, and the gray every inch of the way.

At forty-six, Ellen had managed to keep her trim figure, and people were always surprised to hear she had grown children. Oh, she found a thread of gray in her short, dark curls from time to time, and the brightly lit mirror on her dressing table was ruthless in pointing out the lines that had begun to crease her eyes and the corners of her mouth. But Ellen had never been vain, and she was thankful Jake was diplomatic in overlooking these presages of middle age. He often borrowed the line from an old commercial: "You're not getting older, you're getting better."

How right she had been to marry this man who sat beside her now, waiting to watch their youngest son take his diploma in hand. In the darkness of the auditorium, Ellen reached for Jake's hand and squeezed it.

Jake recognized the faraway look in Ellen's eyes and knew that she was walking through the joyful corridors of their shared history. He looked down the row at his family— now grown and writing their own histories—and he, too, was transported back through the years.

Jake had grown up in the city. His father was a partner in a law firm on Chicago's West Side. Robert Brighton had lived for the firm, or more accurately, at the firm. He kept a foldaway cot in a closet of his large office, and to Jake it seemed he slept there more nights than he slept with Jake's mother. When he did come home there was a stiff silence between husband and wife. Not until Jake was older did he discover that his father's long nights at the office were not always spent alone.

One day when Jake was twelve years old, he suddenly realized he had not seen his father for days. When he asked his mother about it, thinking maybe his father was away on one of his frequent business trips, she told him without emotion, "He's not coming back, Jake. We're getting a divorce." Jake sometimes wondered if she would ever have told him had he not asked.

Jake had wasted many months burning with anger at his father, though not so much because he missed the man, or because he felt cheated out of having a father. His father's absence had changed very little in the family's life. Jake's anger had been on his mother's behalf.

After the divorce, Margaret Brighton seemed to retreat into herself, and from that time on Jake rarely saw her enjoy anything in life. She took a job as a secretary and, as Jake later found out, was well provided for with child support and alimony checks. But gone forever were the gentle laughter and the happy singing he remembered from his boyhood. His mother now lived her days in a dull march of duty that left little room for the special times Jake had enjoyed with her during his early childhood.

Jake didn't see or hear of his father again until his mother mailed the obituary to him his first year at the university. Robert Brighton had suffered a heart attack in the early morning hours on the cot in his office. He was forty-eight years old.

In spite of his somber homelife, Jake was not without happiness. He was well liked at school, a capable student, and a gifted athlete. He had gone to the university on a tennis scholarship. His coaches, however, were frustrated with his seeming lack of motivation to develop his talent to its fullest potential. But Robert Brighton's lust for work and wealth had tempered his son's ambitions, and Jake vowed that whatever he did in life, he would not allow it to become an obsession. He also vowed that, above all, he would be a husband to his wife and a father to his children. He spoke the vow aloud in his cramped room in the dormitory, and then he wadded his father's obituary into a crumpled ball and ceremoniously threw it into the trash.

Though Jake had always thought he would marry someday, he hadn't really been looking for a wife the day Ellen walked into his classroom. He was in his fourth year of teaching, and his life was full and busy with classroom projects, grading papers, and staff meetings. Jake had fallen in love with his students. Having rarely been around young children, he was captivated by his second graders' enthusiasm for the simplest pleasures. He was drawn to their innocent trust in life's goodness.

One of Jake's responsibilities was supervising an early-morning detention hall for kids who couldn't serve time after school. The same group of delinquents seemed to make their way to Jake's classroom every few weeks. These were the kids who especially stole his heart. He ached for them. At seven and eight they seemed so innocent, so full of hope and promise. Some of them were truly bright. In fact, it was their very keenness that sometimes got them into trouble. Their detentions were, for the most part, the result of pranks, tardiness, or occasional cheating. But by the time they were ten or eleven, many were pulled into the sordid world of drugs and gangs that seemed to be the inevitable destination for boys (and not a few girls) of the projects. He saw them on the sidewalks after school making their deals and planning their heists. They recognized him with glazed eyes that often revealed a glimmer of guilt, but gone were the warmth and candor that had existed between Mr. Brighton and his young charges in those morning hours just three years before. When he saw their hardened eyes in faces still soft and whiskerless, and heard their youthful lips uttering ugly curses, he couldn't help feeling as though somehow he had failed them.

It was this he was contemplating the afternoon Ellen came into his classroom the second week of the school year. He stood in his room gazing out the window at a group of boys clustered in front of the old building. So deep in thought was he that she was standing right behind him before he realized anyone had entered the room.

She cleared her throat loudly, and he spun around, startled. Ellen burst out laughing.

"I'm sorry," she said, muffling another giggle. "I didn't mean to scare you like that."

"My fault," he said sheepishly. "I was a million miles away." He regained his composure and stuck out his hand. "I'm Jake Brighton. You teach the kindergarten class down the hall, right?"

She nodded. "Right. Ellen Randolph. I don't remember seeing you at the staff meeting."

"No. I get the honor of monitoring detention hall that time of morning. You'd think we could at least wait till school has been in session for a couple weeks before we start handing out detentions. But I guess they want it known in no uncertain terms that 'violators will be punished.' " He curled his fingers into quote marks and chalked them in the air to emphasize the legalese. "Actually, that's what I was pondering so intently when you scared the daylights out of me."

She smiled. "I'm really sorry about that." Her expression turned serious. "Rough bunch of kids, huh?"

"Oh no, it's not that. Actually, they're some of my favorites. They've got spirit. And really, they're not bad kids . . . not yet anyway. That's what bothers me. I look out there"—he gestured toward the window—"and I see what they have waiting for them a few years down the road, and I wish I could do something to keep them from it."

Her gaze followed his to the unruly group gathered outside. "Yes, I know what you mean," she said. "I grew up on a farm, and I guess I was a little naive. I came here thinking I could make a difference in these kids' lives. But how can I really do anything for them when they are surrounded by bad influences day in and day out? Sometimes I just want to load all my little kindergartners on a bus and take them to the farm and let my mom and dad have them for a few years!"

She smiled, and immediately Jake was drawn to her compassion for these kids he had come to love so much. "Well, if you're an example of what your mom and dad can do with a kid, I'm all for that idea!"

Deep color rose in Ellen's cheeks, and she quickly changed the subject. "I guess I'd better get moving if I'm going to finish all my papers and still catch a bus before dark." She was halfway out the door when she stopped abruptly and put her hand to her mouth, flustered. "Oh! I almost forgot why I came down here in the first place. I was wondering if you have a state map I could borrow for to- morrow morning. I've been up and down the hall and no- body else seems to have one."

"Well, this is your lucky day. I have one—it's kind of an- cient, like everything else around here, but you're welcome to use it. It's heavy, though . . . it's on a roller. Here, I'll show you." He rolled down two or three maps that were mounted like window shades at the back of the room. "Here we are—Illinois. How about if I bring it down to your class- room first thing in the morning?"

"Thanks a lot. I'd appreciate that." She turned to go. "See you around, Mr. Brighton."

I hope so, Jake thought as he watched Ellen walk down the hallway.

The next morning as soon as his detention class had been dismissed, he took the map to her classroom. She was standing on a chair tacking some of the children's artwork high on a bulletin board. He purposely sneaked up behind her and then cleared his throat loudly. She gasped and lost her balance. Her arms flailed in the air as involuntarily and ungracefully she leapt from the chair to keep from falling. When she righted herself and saw that it was Jake, she burst out laughing at her own exaggerated antics. She blushingly conceded, "Well, I guess I had that coming!"

He put a steadying hand on her shoulder. "Yes, you did," he exhorted. Then apologetically he added, "But I really didn't mean to knock you off the chair. Are you okay?"

"I'm fine. It served me right." She shook a finger play- fully in his face. "But you do it again, and I'll send you to the principal's office, young man!"

He laughed. "I'll bet you've got a reputation around

here already. Mean ol' Miss Randolph."

"Well, I'm working on it. It's 'kids' like you who turn perfectly nice teachers like me into old crabs, you know."

Jake was taken with her lighthearted teasing and those smiling blue-gray eyes.

"Hey! Do you like Chinese food?" he asked impulsively.

"Well, to tell you the truth I've never tasted it, unless you count the chow mein in a can that my mom used to make when there was nothing else in the cupboards."

Jake shook his head. "That doesn't count. Listen, there's a place in Calypso, where I live, that makes the greatest Chinese this side of the globe. Would you like to go there with me Friday night?"

She flashed a smile. "Friday? I'd like that. What time?"

"Would you mind leaving from here after school? It takes almost an hour on the bus. I don't have a car yet," he said apologetically.

"I don't mind the bus, really. I'm just not too crazy about taking it back into the city late at night."

"Oh, don't worry; I'll ride back with you. My mom lives on the West Side, and I can stay with her if it's too late."

"It's a date, then. I'll wait here for you after school."

Jake turned and started to leave the room, then he laughed and held up the unwieldy rolled-up map. "We seem to have trouble accomplishing what we intend to when we get in each other's classrooms!"

Ellen laughed with him, took the map, and walked to the front of her classroom as chattering kindergartners began to take their places around the tables in the spacious room.

Friday nights in Calypso became a standing date for Jake and Ellen. The Friday-night special at The China Garden was egg foo yong, and it was so exquisite that they rarely ventured another choice. Jake had never felt so comfortable with a girl before. Not that Ellen was just "comfortable"—

Jake was incredibly attracted to her, but he was afraid if he brought romance into the picture he might lose the best friend he'd ever had.

He could talk to Ellen about anything. She listened to his ideas, and understood his feelings like no one he had ever known. He shared with her parts of himself that he had never let anyone else even get close to, and he did it with no qualms or hesitation. He trusted Ellen. It was a new experience for Jake, having grown up in such a silent home, to be sharing every thought and feeling.

And while Ellen tended to be quiet and reserved in social situations, with him she was vocal and exuberant. Their time together was punctuated by joking and teasing. Jake had never known there could be so much to laugh at in the world.

The hour on the bus from the city each week was spent in rapt conversation. Jake told Ellen his whole life story, and her compassion soothed the pain of his past. She in turn opened up her life to him. Together they mulled over problems they each encountered with their students; they analyzed the world and everything in it; and somewhere along Eden's Expressway, Jake knew he was in love with her.

Their wedding ceremony was on a hot August evening. Illinois was parched and dusty in the midst of a drought that had brought creases of worry to Howard Randolph's forehead. But Jake saw the worry change to pride as the older man brought his daughter to meet Jake at the altar of the little country church.

It was a brief ceremony, beautiful in its very simplicity. Ellen looked trustingly into Jake's eyes as he spoke to her the vows that a myriad of couples through the centuries had spoken.

"I, Jake, take thee, Ellen, to be my lawful wedded wife. To have and to hold from this day forward, for better or for worse, for richer, for poorer, in sickness and in health, to love and to cherish, and to thee only will I cleave, as long as we both shall live."

And Ellen, lovely in her grandmother's gown, ivory with age, echoed the troth in a voice strong and full of confidence.

Ellen's parents gave the newlyweds money for a motel in Springfield and loaned them their car for the trip. They drove away from the church, replete with promise for the life they would live together. Over and over they said to each other, "Can you believe it? We're really married!" And they manufactured excuses to say "my husband" and "my wife."

It was after midnight when they finally found the motel. It was on the edge of town and had seen better days. The paint was peeling inside and out, and the curtains and bedspread were something from the thirties—"the dirty thirties," Jake had joked.

But the yearning and passion and pure love that burned in their hearts that night as they became one in body and spirit belied the humble room they shared.

They came home from their meager honeymoon to the little attic apartment that Jake had been renting for three years before their marriage. The apartment was in Calypso, a small suburb west of Chicago. The house sat on an oak-canopied avenue not far from the main street of town, but the expansive yard and surrounding woods gave it the feel of an old country home.

The house was owned by Oscar and Hattie Miles. After three years, this lively gray-headed couple had become the doting parents Jake never had.

Jake tried to concentrate on the program in the stuffy auditorium, but his thoughts kept replaying the past twenty-five years. As the graduation speaker droned on, he thought fondly of his dear friends Oscar and Hattie. Oh, how he missed them! And how much they had given to him. He would have given anything if that dear couple could be here sharing this graduation day with Kyle. They had been gone for several years, but Jake saw their faces before him now, indelibly etched in a cherished niche in his memory.

Oscar Miles had immigrated to the States with his parents and three younger sisters when he was fourteen years old. His family had owned a prosperous textile mill in London, but when his mother became ill, his father had sold his share of the business to his brothers and brought his family to America, where he was assured his wife would receive the best of medical care. Oscar's mother recovered, and the family thrived in the new country.

Though Oscar was American through and through, having proudly become a citizen on his twenty-first birthday, he retained the charm and genteel ways of an Englishman, punctuated by the trace of London that lingered in his deep voice.

Hattie was plump and cheerful, and with her halo of white hair she reminded Jake of an angel. He spent almost as much time in Hattie's fragrant kitchen as he did in his own apartment. Hattie derived great delight in baking tarts, pies, and the English scones her mother-in-law had taught her to make. Her special pastries gave Jake great pleasure as well. But when the bathroom scale showed he had added eight pounds to his frame in as many months, he begged her to quit tempting him. She just gave her musical chuckle and plopped another spoonful of blackberry cobbler onto his plate.

It was at Hattie's table that Jake had found true meaning in his life. For she had shown him God.

Jake had always believed in the concept of God. He had never understood how man could see nature—the beauty of the landscape, the perfection of the workings of the human body, the amazing cycle of life—and not believe in God on some level. But Hattie *knew* God. God was as real and as personal to her as Oscar was. She spoke *of* this God and *to* Him as easily as she spoke of and to her husband. Jake listened to her stories—her testimonies—of an intimate God of love, and he wanted to believe. One night, after Oscar shared his own stories of faith—faith in a living God through His Son Jesus Christ—Jake could no longer find a reason not to believe.

It was that night Jake found healing for the pain of an absent father and a distant mother. He found meaning for his work with the children at school and a reason to hope for their future, as well as his own.

The Mileses' only daughter had died of cancer two years before Jake moved into the apartment. They told Jake often that he was God's gift to them in their sorrow. The responsibility of being "sent from God" to these people weighed heavily on him, but they were such a blessing to him that he never wanted to disappoint them.

Oscar and Hattie were ecstatic when Jake announced his engagement to Ellen. When he told them they wanted to keep the apartment after their marriage, Oscar proceeded to paint the kitchen and have new carpeting put in the living room. Hattie all but banished Jake from the place while she scrubbed floors and washed windows.

With Ellen's collection of furniture from the farm, and Jake's mishmash acquired at garage sales and flea markets, the apartment soon became a quaint and cozy haven. The two spent leisurely afternoons browsing flea markets and dusty antique shops, finding just the right touches to make the rooms of the apartment their own. Jake taught Ellen the fine art of bargaining, and within a few weeks, she was wheedling the stingiest of proprietors into incredible deals.

Ellen reveled in making curtains and pillows for the tiny bedroom and drove Jake crazy arranging and rearranging the furniture.

Ellen sighed and shifted in her seat. The commencement speaker was telling these young men and women, ready to make their way into the world, that anything was possible. "Reach for your dreams . . ." he urged them. "Set high goals, and don't let any obstacle keep you from reaching them. . . ."

Ah, she thought, *but sometimes things are beyond our control.* She and Jake had made lofty plans. Starry-eyed, they had lain awake late into the nights dreaming and scheming and timing everything to perfection. But Providence had taken them down a different path.

Jake and Ellen had come back from their honeymoon to their teaching jobs at North Lawndale. Just after Christmas, completely contrary to their schedule, Ellen began to suspect that she might be pregnant. She was only a few days late, but her body had taken on a new fullness, and the queasiness in her stomach on the bus each morning became more and more difficult to ignore. She and Jake had talked often about the children they would someday have, but both had agreed that they wanted to have more than the tiny apartment and teachers' salaries to offer their babies. They hadn't even felt they could afford a car yet, though Oscar had been generous in lending them his.

Ellen was afraid to tell Jake her suspicions. He was so careful with their money and had such a precise plan set out: teach another year, buy a car, then go back to school for his master's degree so he could find a job that would allow Ellen to quit teaching and have their babies. It was a good plan—a reasonable plan. But as Ellen became sure that she was indeed going to have a baby, she became increasingly unreasonable in her joy over the fact. She thought of nothing else. She decorated nurseries in her dreams and even bought a book of babies' names. This she hid under her side of the bed and looked at it furtively and guiltily while Jake was in the shower or out playing tennis. She began to feel dishonest keeping this momentous news from the one who had helped make it so, but, after all, it had not yet been confirmed by a doctor.

Three weeks passed and still her period had not come, and the morning nausea was getting worse. She would have to tell Jake sooner or later. She was so afraid he would blame her—or worse, that he would grow to blame the baby for making such a drastic revision to their well-planned blueprint.

Finally she made an appointment at the county health clinic to have a pregnancy test. She realized as she sat in the reception room waiting for the results that she was now more afraid of *not* being pregnant than of being so. She desperately wanted the little life she was certain grew inside her.

A nurse, a woman of about fifty with graying hair and a no-nonsense manner, appeared in the doorway. She motioned to Ellen and led her to a small room at the end of the hall.

"Well, Mrs. Brighton, you are indeed pregnant. I hope that's good news." She glanced suspiciously at Ellen's plain gold wedding band. "Of course you'll need to make an appointment with your doctor to determine an accurate due date and make sure everything is progressing as it should."

She gave Ellen a small stack of pamphlets to read. Ellen thanked her, gathered her coat and purse, and made her way down the corridor that led to the street. She had walked the rather long distance from the apartment, and now, in spite of the biting cold, she welcomed the time it would take her to get home.

As the confirmation of her suspicions sank in, Ellen was filled not with apprehension but with the purest joy she had ever known. She was carrying the child of the man she loved more than anyone or anything in the world. She wanted to turn cartwheels and shout at the top of her lungs. She felt invincible. They would find a way around any obstacles to have this child. Their humble plans suddenly seemed insignificant in the face of this new life they had created.

But as each step took her closer to the apartment, her confidence dwindled, and by the time she opened their front door the joy had been pushed out by uncertainty.

Jake was sitting at the small table in the kitchen, reading the paper. They couldn't afford a subscription to *The Tribune*, but Oscar and Hattie shared their newspaper with them each day. Jake looked up and opened his mouth to speak, when Ellen, much to her own astonishment, burst into tears.

"Oh, Jake, I'm pregnant!" she wailed.

His face registered shock, but no words came from his gaping mouth. He pushed the newspaper to the floor and stood up hesitantly. Then he gathered Ellen in his arms and held her as great sobs wracked her thin frame. They stood that way for long minutes until finally Jake found his voice. "Ellen, are you sure?"

"Yes, I'm sure," she spat through gulping sobs. "I just had a test at the clinic. Oh, Jake, I'm sorry. I thought I was so careful."

He held her at arm's length. "Ellen, is it that terrible? I mean, are you okay? Everything's all right, isn't it?" There was worry in his voice now.

"Everything's okay with the baby, but look what I've done, Jake. How will you ever go back to school now? How will we buy a car? We don't even have a place to put the baby. Oh, Jake, I didn't time this very well." And she dissolved into tears again.

"Well, excuse me, Mrs. Brighton, but if I have my facts straight, I get a little credit for all this too!"

Ellen smiled through her tears. "Oh, Jake, just think—a baby! I've worried so much that you'd be upset . . . but, honey, I'm so happy. I can't help it. I want this baby—more than you can imagine."

Jake was thoughtful for a moment. "You've been acting really strange the last couple weeks. I thought there was something wrong between us. But now it all makes sense . . . how long have you known?"

"I started to get suspicious right after Christmas, but I didn't know for sure until the test today. Jake, I've been so happy thinking about this baby, I would have been crushed if the test had been negative. Is that awful of me?"

"Honey, it's . . . it's wonderful! So we'll have to change our plans a little. Will it really make any difference twenty years from now that we got a little behind on our big financial schedule? Oh, Ellen, I'm just relieved that this is what has been eating you. I've felt like you were a million miles away, and I couldn't figure out what I had done. It all makes sense now." His tone turned stern. "But you should have told me. Don't you ever keep anything this important from me, El." Softening, he took her face tenderly in his hands and touched his nose to hers. "I love you, Ellen Brighton," he said fiercely, crushing her to himself. "Our baby will have the most beautiful mother in the world. This is a blessing." He spoke the words like a decree.

Catherine MaryEllen Brighton was born August 17 at five o'clock in the afternoon. After twelve hours of labor Ellen had given birth with relative ease, but as soon as the doctor announced it was a girl, the nurses whisked the baby out of the room with grim faces. Ellen's and Jake's questions went unanswered, but they knew something was terribly wrong. Ellen slept fitfully with Jake holding her hand. She awoke to Jake's gentle nudging and the doctor's low voice.

"I'm so sorry," the doctor said simply. "Your baby died a few minutes ago. She was born with a severe heart defect, and we did everything we could for her, but there was really never any hope." He paused, waiting for a response. Met with silence, he continued. "It was nothing you did . . . nothing you could have known or done anything about. Please don't blame yourselves. This is a very rare occurrence, and there's no reason you cannot have another healthy baby when Mrs. Brighton has recovered sufficiently."

Though Ellen was lying flat in the bed, the room was spinning, and an oddly hushed buzzing began to pound in her head. In the hour since the baby's birth, she had tried to prepare herself for the possibility of this news, and had prayerfully, painfully given the child into God's hands. But now the uncertain fear had become a cruel reality. The baby they had dreamed about, planned for, and waited nine endless months for was gone before they could hold her in their arms. They had loved this baby before they had even felt her move within Ellen's belly. Ellen felt the emptiness like a deep abyss. It was too much to bear. How could the doctor even speak about another baby? How could anyone be expected to survive such grief?

Jake sat in a straight chair beside Ellen's hospital bed. He had barely moved from this place for almost fourteen hours. Through a haze of grief Ellen watched him sitting there, his head buried in his hands, but she was too numb to reach out to him.

Then suddenly summoning strength, she spoke, her

voice fierce. "I want to see my baby."

"Mrs. Brighton . . ." The doctor grasped for words. "Do you . . . do you understand that your baby is gone?"

"I understand. I just want to hold her one time." Her voice broke. "Please don't deny me that."

The doctor hesitated. "All right. It will be some time before they can bring her up to your room, but I'll let them know your wishes." The doctor made a scribbled note on Ellen's chart and left the room.

At twilight a nurse brought the baby to Ellen's room. The young woman—no older than Ellen—was teary-eyed and unable to speak, but she put the bundle gently in Ellen's arms and left the young couple alone.

They had dressed her in a tiny undershirt and booties and wrapped her in a soft pink blanket. Her face was translucent as fine porcelain, with blue veins tracing a pale web. She was perfect. She had fine dark hair that curled around her neck and forehead. "Like yours, Ellen," Jake said. And his saying so was a gift.

For half an hour they held their baby and marveled at her beauty. They counted her fingers and toes. They called her by her name and told her they loved her. And they said goodbye. It was almost more than they could bear when the nurse came and took the baby from Ellen's arms and carried her forever from their lives. But Jake and Ellen never regretted having spent that sacred time with their firstborn. They often spoke of it as a blessing, and they were to look back on those moments as the beginning of their healing.

They buried Catherine in a tiny white coffin under an ancient oak tree in the Randolph family plot. The cemetery was a peaceful, secluded place in the country. It sat on a hill behind Ellen's childhood church, surrounded protectively by a wrought-iron fence. As children, Ellen and her sisters had scaled the fence and played hide-and-seek there while their parents visited after Sunday services. It comforted Ellen to think of their baby in a setting from her own childhood.

Jake and Ellen stayed with the Randolphs until the weekend. Ellen was feeling strong physically, though the fullness of her breasts and the dwindling flow of blood were constant reminders of how recently her baby had been cradled warm and safe in her womb. But it was heartening to be pampered by her mother and her sisters, and it was a bittersweet pleasure to share the farm with Jake. They walked in the fields and along the country roads for hours, praying together, talking out their feelings, and planning how they would go on with their lives after this bitter disappointment. And somehow in spite of the sorrow, they knew there was a blessing hidden somewhere in the pain. They had a child in heaven. No one could take away the love that had grown in their hearts for this child, or the bond that had melded them together through the joy and the sorrow and the hope.

When they got back to Calypso, Oscar and Hattie were there to offer their sympathy. They enveloped Jake and Ellen in warm hugs.

"The good Lord has a reason for everything, child," Hattie told Ellen. "Just give Him time and He'll take care of the hurt. I speak from experience, you know. Time and God are mighty healers . . . you'll see."

There were the nursery things tucked in the corner of the bedroom to deal with. On the first night they were back, Jake carried the cradle down to Oscar's garage and then came up and sat on the bed as Ellen folded the blankets and packed the tiny sleepers and gowns into a cardboard box.

Ellen warmed a can of tomato soup and set a package of stale saltines on the table, but they ate little. They prepared for bed wordlessly and fell asleep, exhausted, in each other's arms.

Ellen awoke several hours later to find Jake's side of the bed empty. Seeing the bathroom light was off, she padded silently into the living room and found him hunched over the desk, his head on his arms. At first she thought he had fallen asleep, but as she moved toward him she saw his shoulders heave and fall. And then she heard him. She stood there in agony, frozen, unable to move, while her husband sobbed like a child. Not knowing how to comfort him, she crept back to bed and lay quietly, sick at heart, until she finally heard him wash his face and come to bed. He pulled her to himself, not realizing she was fully awake. They lay together, her body curved to his, like nesting spoons, until at last she felt his even breaths on the back of her neck and knew he slept. She lay awake till dawn, aching more for her husband than for the child they had lost.

Yes, there had been sorrowful times early in their marriage. And though it was a tired cliché, time and God really did heal all their wounds. Catherine's death would forever be a tender memory, but Jake and Ellen found comfort in the psalmist's words, "Joy comes in the morning."

After Catherine's death, Jake and Ellen's joy had come in the form of three more children, each one as precious as the child they had lost. Jake smiled proudly now as his youngest son stepped up to the podium to receive his diploma. Glancing at Ellen, whose tears sparkled in her eyes, Jake squeezed her hand. It was as if they were sharing the years together—silently, but as one.

Jake was struck anew by the truth of Hattie's words spoken so many years earlier: "Time and God are mighty healers."

It had been a long road back to happiness, though. After Catherine's death, Ellen had been immersed in a dark depression that threatened to also drown Jake as he struggled to pull her out of its murky waters. She went through her days at school like an automaton. Jake could see that she made an effort to be cheerful for his sake, but her laughter rang false, and he would often find her staring into nothingness, oblivious to his words and his comfort. He heard her cry out to God, begging to know why. He knew she struggled to find the blessing they had felt so sure was hidden in Catherine's death.

The doctor had said they could try for another baby after three months, but when Jake broached the subject with Ellen, she tersely said she wasn't ready yet and closed the topic by leaving the room. Jake began to fear that Ellen would never recover.

She had seemed so strong in the first days after Catherine's death. But when they returned to their classrooms, and life resumed its routine, a gloom had enveloped her. Terrifyingly, her behavior began to remind him of his mother's in the days after his father had left them. The same vacant stare, the self-absorbed manner. Ellen seemed indifferent to his personal grief as had his mother to his adolescent misery. But he could not find it in himself to be angry with her. He knew that though he felt the loss of their child deeply, his heartache was more the result of disappointment—the death of a dream. He had not carried their child under his heart for nine months; he had not felt her tiny arms and legs fluttering inside him. He had not suffered the travail of giving birth, only to have the reward of such pain snatched away so cruelly. He felt he could not deny Ellen license to rail against whatever had willed her this cross. So he kept silent. And the silence was a brash echo in their little apartment under the eaves.

But a year after they had buried Catherine, Ellen was pregnant again. Once more, the pregnancy had not been planned, but Jake hoped beyond hope that this baby would bring back the glow to Ellen's face.

For the first few months Ellen's eyes were filled with fear, but suddenly as if a dam had broken, instead of holding her feelings inside, she lay awake late into the nights talking and talking with Jake. As Ellen confided her darkest fears to her husband, he watched them evaporate like dew in the sun, to be replaced with tiny buds of hope.

That such profound sorrow could be replaced by such great joy was a mystery he would never truly comprehend. But he reasoned that perhaps one could not feel happiness with such depth if one had not first known the fathoms of anguish.

When Jana Beth's first lusty cries filled the delivery room, and the doctor placed her, whole and perfect, on Ellen's belly, Jake watched the last remnant of her grief vanish, and it was as though Ellen herself was the one newly born—hope having given full bloom to joy. Though she confided to Jake that she would never truly understand why Catherine had been taken from them, Ellen acknowledged that Jana's birth had restored her faith in the God to whom she had entrusted her life. And now she ran confidently back into His arms.

As grief and heartache had been the hallmark of the first year of their marriage, the succeeding years had been full of exultant joy and great hope for the future.

Shortly after Jana's birth, Jake applied for a position as Calypso's elementary school principal. It was a coveted position, and he had little hope of even being considered for the job. To their amazement, he was offered the job with only one stipulation—that he take a few courses at the university to comply with the qualifications. Ellen and Jake were elated. Now not only would he have a job in the suburbs, but also he would have financial assistance in working toward the degree he had planned to get anyway. And the new salary would boost the meager bank account they had struggled with since Ellen quit teaching to be home with Jana.

They borrowed three thousand dollars from Howard and MaryEllen and put a down payment on a little house three blocks from Oscar and Hattie's. The house needed painting inside and out, and the yard was a tangle of weeds, but it was structurally sound and more importantly, it was theirs. They spent their weekends raking and seeding the lawn, and by the time school started, the grass was green and lush and the backyard had been enclosed with a rough board fence. The inside of the house could wait until winter.

Now as their precious little girl toddled across their hearts, another little life waited to make "his" entrance into their world. Jake had a feeling that this was his boy.

Brant Allen Brighton was born in January, and much to their surprise, Kyle Andrew followed along only fourteen months later.

How they treasured their little family! Jake came home each day to the happy sounds of laughter. Sometimes in the evening Jake watched Ellen playing with the children when she was unaware of his gaze, and it filled him with joy to see this demonstration of his wife's happiness. Her days as a young mother at home were full and busy, and she declared her contentment often to Jake.

Then, when Kyle started first grade, Ellen went back to school, teaching second grade at Calypso Elementary. Teaching had allowed her to be home when her own children were, and Jake knew that it, too, brought her deep fulfillment.

Jake served as principal of Calypso Elementary for almost ten years. He had worked his way through graduate school, taking night classes and summer school. It was a challenge, trying to juggle a demanding career, graduate classes, and a young family, but when Jake was promoted to the position of high school principal, and seven years later was offered the position of superintendent of schools, it all seemed worthwhile.

Their life had been full of blessings. As he sat at this crossroads in his life, Jake took stock, numbering the gifts the Lord had bestowed on them.

Their children were all happy and healthy and finding their places in life. Kyle already knew that he wanted to teach—a decision that thrilled his parents. And Brant was happy at the university.

Jana had married her college sweetheart, Mark McFarlane, and they both had good jobs in the city.

Ellen's parents were still living on the farm, and though their age was beginning to slow them down a bit, they remained healthy and active.

Margaret Brighton had died suddenly last summer. But her last decade had been almost a redemption of the years Jake's father had taken from her. She doted on her grandchildren, and when she was with them, Jake often caught a glimpse of the lighthearted woman that had once been his mother.

Oscar and Hattie had died within a year of each other, just a year before Jake's promotion. It was this more than anything that made Jake and Ellen feel they had stepped into new roles. It seemed strange that they were becoming the older generation; neither of them was quite comfortable in the role yet. Oh, time had flown so quickly. Was it possible that their last tiny baby was all grown up and nearly on his own? Today's commencement marked a new beginning not just for Kyle, but for his parents as well. . . .

The bright lights of the auditorium came up, and the

swell of the recessional signaled the end of the ceremony. Jake and Ellen turned and smiled at each other, their reveries broken. Kyle winked at his parents as he walked up the aisle with a bounce in his step. And with that, the last little bird was pushed from the nest.

2

    Ellen kicked off her shoes and with a weary but satisfied sigh slumped into a plump, overstuffed chair in the living room. From her perch, she could see through to the brightly lit kitchen. The sink overflowed with dirty dishes, the countertops were littered with half-empty glasses and crumpled napkins, and the floor was a collage of various crumbs and spills.

    The last of the guests had just left Kyle's graduation party, and the rest of the family had retreated to the deck in the backyard, leaving Ellen in a quiet but messy house. It had been a wonderful party, and Ellen didn't begrudge the work she had ahead of her. But she was exhausted.

    The back door swung open and Jana appeared in the doorway. Boisterous male voices drifted in on the night air. The men of the family were in a heated discussion about the predicted outcome of a postseason tournament.

    Jana caught her mother's eye and rolled her own eyes toward the ceiling. "There's too much testosterone out there," she declared. A burst of raucous laughter from the deck was cut off abruptly as she closed the door behind her.

Ellen laughed. "Well, you'd better decide which is worse. Testosterone out there, or a sinkful of dirty dishes in here."

Jana looked the kitchen over. "Ugh! Tough choice." But she pushed up her sleeves and came over to where Ellen was sitting in the living room. "Okay . . . let's get it over with." She took her mother by both hands and playfully hauled her out of the chair. They walked into the kitchen arm in arm.

Together they cleared off the counters; then Ellen rinsed the dishes while Jana loaded the dishwasher.

"I'm glad you and Mark decided to stay overnight," Ellen told her daughter.

"Oh sure, you're just happy to have help with the dishes," Jana teased.

Ellen smiled. "Well, that too. But seriously, I know it means a lot to Kyle to have you and Mark here tonight."

"I'm glad we stayed, too, Mom. It's been a fun evening. We would have been too tired to drive back tonight anyway."

The two worked in comfortable silence for a while. Then Jana mused, "Didn't Kyle look cute up there tonight? I just can't believe my baby brother has graduated!"

"I can't believe my baby graduated. . . ." Just then Kyle came in through the back door. Ellen smiled mischievously. ". . . and speaking of my baby—here he is, just in time to help with the dishes." Kyle did an about-face and tried to escape through the still-open door. His sister grabbed him by the arm and dragged him back into the house. Ellen watched their lighthearted exchange wistfully. It was so good to have everyone home together—just like the old days.

The rest of the men straggled in from outdoors. Jake came up behind Ellen at the sink and rubbed her aching shoulders.

Her hands still in dishwater, she closed her eyes, relishing the massage. "Mmm . . . don't stop . . . that feels great. But you guys picked a bad time to come in." She tossed a dishrag over her shoulder in Brant's direction. "Here . . . wipe that counter off, will you?" Brant wadded the rag into a wet ball and threw it at Kyle. Kyle, in turn, lobbed it across the room to Mark. Even Jake got in on the "hot potato" game until things got so rowdy that Ellen, only half kidding, hollered in protest.

"Hey, you guys! Cut it out!"

Jake took charge. "Come on, guys. Let's help your mother out. Brant, will you get those leaves out of the table? And, Kyle, you can carry these folding chairs out to the garage."

Twenty minutes later, the kitchen was spotless, and Brant and Kyle were raiding the refrigerator for a midnight snack. Kyle spied a leftover corner of his decorated graduation cake, covered with foil.

"Anybody care if I finish this off?"

"Just so you wash your dishes when you're through," Ellen sighed.

Kyle grabbed a fork and came over to where she was standing. He leaned his elbow heavily on her shoulder, using her for a "table" while he fed himself man-sized bites of the cake. He was a head taller than his mother and outweighed her by at least seventy pounds. This was her baby! It didn't seem possible!

"Good party, Mom . . . thanks," he mumbled through a mouthful of frosting.

"It was fun, wasn't it?"

"Did you get some good pictures at graduation, Dad?"

Ellen intercepted the question. "Oh, very funny, Kyle," she said with sarcasm. "So help me, if you look like Howdy Doody in all your pictures, I'll wring your neck!" She demonstrated just how she would do it, and grinning impishly, Kyle ducked out of her grasp and ran up the stairs to his room.

"Good-night, everybody," he hollered down behind him. "Thanks for all the loot. . . ."

"Good-night, Kyle . . . you're welcome," they said in unison.

"Good-night, honey . . . love you." Oh, how she would miss that boy!

Jake and Ellen stood in the driveway watching Kyle's little Toyota round the curve and disappear out of sight. It had been a tearful but joyful goodbye. Kyle was so excited about being on his own he could hardly wait to be on the road. New Mexico was far away, but in a few weeks he would be closer to home in Urbana. Kyle's enthusiasm was contagious, and his parents found themselves smiling in spite of the poignancy of the moment.

The morning was chilly for June, but the birds were singing and the sky was clear. They started to walk back up to the house, arm in arm.

"Well, Mrs. Brighton. Looks like it's just you and me."

"Are you trying to make me cry again?"

"No, ma'am. Actually, I kind of like the sound of it . . . just the two of us. No phone ringing off the hook, no doors slamming, actual food in the refrigerator. Why, we might even be able to finish a conversation in one sitting."

She leaned her head on his shoulder and sighed contentedly. "Won't that be nice."

They stood in the driveway looking up at the big house.

Jake sighed. "I wish Oscar and Hattie could see how the kids have turned out. They'd be pleased this house has held so much happiness for us."

The Mileses had been like grandparents to the Brighton children, and Jake had taken their deaths hard. However, they had left a tangible legacy to the family when they willed the beautiful house on West Oaklawn to Jake. For the growing Brighton family, the gift of the house was almost too good to be true. The fact that their fortune came as a result of their dearest friends' deaths tempered their joy—tinged it with unwarranted guilt even. Oscar and Hattie were sorely missed, and the house hardly made up for the loss of their love and their wisdom. But they had left a legacy of happy memories that would always be a part of Jake.

Before moving into the old house, Jake and Ellen had spent many hours refinishing woodwork, painting, and wallpapering. The kitchen had been completely remodeled, and a modest conservatory was fashioned out of the summer porch behind the kitchen. It was exhausting work that took the better part of a year to complete, but when Jake and Ellen stepped over the threshold the day the last piece of furniture was in place, they felt they had come full circle. There was a bedroom for each of the children on the second floor, and Jake and Ellen appropriated the attic—their first home—as a master suite, complete with bathroom, sitting room, and kitchenette. It was hard to believe that they had once lived solely in this tiny space, but it made a wonderful hideaway from the stresses of teaching children all day and coming home to three of their own.

Jake remembered with a smile the day they had moved in. He had carried Ellen over the threshold of their bedroom suite, and the attic above 245 West Oaklawn had been consecrated by their love and union.

Now, having ushered the last of their children out of that house, they stood at the entrance to the back door, each apprehensive about facing the emptiness within. Jake reached to turn the knob but suddenly changed his mind.

"Want to go for a walk? The morning's too pretty to waste."

"Okay. Let me change my shoes and get a jacket."

They set out along West Oaklawn at a brisk pace. They usually walked together in the evenings, and the street looked different in the early morning light. The leaves still wore the yellow-green of spring, and in the dawning sunlight the flower gardens glimmered with dew. It was easy to feel optimistic in this pristine world.

Ellen sighed. "Kyle seems so happy. I hope his job goes as well as he thinks it will. I always worry that he's not very realistic about life."

"He is kind of a Pollyanna," Jake conceded, "but I think I'd rather have him that way than have him as serious as Brant was about everything. Remember what a lost soul he was before he left for college?"

"Oh, Jake, I'd almost forgotten about that. He's so different now."

Brant had been the most rebellious of their three, but now he was finding his place in life. He was in his element at the university. He had found his niche in computer science and had a job that he loved in the computer department on campus. And he was in love. He had brought Cynthia Riley home to meet the family just two weeks before, and they could sense that there was something special between the two.

Ellen was quiet for a minute, deep in thought. "Cynthia has been good for Brant, and I hope he doesn't let her get away. He's grown up so much in the past year, I can't help feeling I've lost my little boy." Then she said, almost to herself, "I guess you're right. Kyle will find his way, too."

They walked in silence for a while.

"We did a good job, didn't we, El?" Jake asked pensively.

She looked at him, questioning in her eyes. "With the kids? I'm so proud of them I could just pop sometimes. We did have some help though, Jake," she teased. "I think the Lord should probably get a little credit."

He took her teasing rebuke seriously. "Oh, I know, I know. I don't see how people raise kids without the Lord. I'm so grateful we started our marriage with Him. I know it doesn't pay to look back, but I can't help wondering how different my own childhood would have been if my parents had known the Lord. It's hard enough when you are a Christian. You know, I look at the families enrolling their children in kindergarten, and I don't envy them a bit. I mean, I know they have some of the best years of their lives ahead, but I have to say I'm thankful that we've done our job and can heave a sigh of relief."

"Jake!" She sounded almost exasperated. "I don't think I'll ever feel like I can quit worrying. I still worry about Jana, even though she has a wonderful husband, a job she loves, a nice apartment. There's just so much that could happen." A new thought came to her. "And just when we think we can quit worrying about Mark and Jana, we'll have grandchildren to worry about! I'm not holding my breath for that, though. I'm afraid they're both too wrapped up in their careers and—"

"You worry too much, Mama," Jake interrupted. He tousled her hair playfully.

"You're right, of course. I know Mark and Jana are very happy together, and I have to let them live their own lives. Kyle too. I know he'll learn more if we let him make a few mistakes. I guess I just feel like worrying is part of my job description."

"Well, don't look now, but the job description just changed."

"I can handle that, I guess. But it's going to feel strange, and it might take some getting used to."

They circled the neighborhood and ended up back in their driveway.

"Let's celebrate our freedom. Breakfast at Perkins?" Jake asked.

"Mmm. Sounds great. Beat you to the shower!"

She shot him a mischievous grin and took off running. Jake easily overtook her, and they pushed and shoved their way up to the attic, Ellen squealing like a schoolgirl. They ended up sharing the shower, laughing and carefree.

Half an hour later they climbed into the car and headed toward the restaurant. Ellen watched her husband as he concentrated on the heavy morning traffic. Her throat was full as she thought how wonderful it was to look forward to the rest of her life with this man.

Oh, she and Jake had their disagreements and misunderstandings. Jake could be incredibly stubborn, and he had an irritating tendency toward perfectionism. But after twenty-four years, their conversations still sparkled, and her heart still skipped a beat when he walked in the back door each evening after work. She could think of no one she would rather be marooned on a desert island with than this man who was her husband, her friend, her lover. Suddenly, the empty nest felt wonderfully full.

⊗∞⊗

Six weeks later Jake found Ellen in the shower at one o'clock in the morning. Neither of them gave it much thought until it happened again a few weeks later. Only this time, Ellen was dressed for work and almost out the door before Jake discovered her and sent her back to bed.

Ellen had been feeling tired and run-down, and at first she thought maybe that explained her strange awakenings.

She told Jake, "I don't know why I don't check the clock before I get out of bed."

She didn't know why, except that her usual morning routine involved slamming the alarm off, heading blindly for the shower, and not opening her eyes until the hot spray hit her face.

She was a few months overdue for her annual physical, so she scheduled an appointment with her doctor. She intended to mention the incidents to Dr. Morton, but by the time she sat on the edge of the examining table, vulnerable and covered only by the flimsy white gown, it seemed like a silly thing to bother him with. To her surprise, he brought the subject up.

"Let's see, Ellen. How old are you now?" He leafed through her chart.

"This is strictly confidential," she teased. Jerry Morton had been their family physician for almost twenty years, and Ellen was comfortable joking with him. "I'll be forty-seven next month."

"Are you still getting your periods regularly?"

"Like clockwork."

"Any problems with hot flashes or night sweats?"

She shook her head. What was he suggesting?

He went on. "Moodiness? Sleeplessness?"

"No . . . well, actually, I have been waking up in the middle of the night once in a while. It's no big deal, except ordinarily I sleep like a log. I've felt kind of run-down lately, so I just attributed it to that." She didn't tell him that her waking up included getting dressed for work, oblivious to the time.

"Well, it's possible this could be the beginnings of menopause."

Ellen was almost shocked. She hadn't thought about

that possibility. She wasn't even forty-seven, for heaven's sake.

Dr. Morton gave her a pamphlet and explained some of the symptoms she might experience over the next months. But otherwise, Ellen left his office with a clean bill of health.

───✦───

Two weeks later, on the last day of August, something very disconcerting happened.

Ellen had had the same classroom at Calypso Elementary for ten years, but when she walked through the front doors on the first day of school she suddenly didn't know which way to turn. She had been to the building several times in the weeks before school started, decorating bulletin boards and arranging the desks in her classroom. But suddenly, everything looked different. The halls were full of noisy, excited children and parents. Ellen went blank. She looked to the left and saw nothing familiar, so she turned right. She walked down the hallway looking into each classroom. She had the strangest feeling that she had somehow gotten in the wrong building. She wasn't even sure why she was in this place. At the end of the hallway, she turned around and started back the other direction. A friendly voice greeted her.

"Ellen! Did you lose somebody already?" She recognized Ginger Barkley, a fourth-grade teacher.

"As a matter of fact, I'm lost."

"Why? Did they switch classrooms on you?"

"Well, no. At least I don't think so."

Ginger looked puzzled. She pointed to the other hallway. "You're still in the east hall, aren't you?"

Ellen tried to cover up her confusion. She laughed nervously. "Oh, I'm just getting my exercise." *What is wrong with me? She must think I'm crazy. I can't understand how that happened. Strange . . .*

She hurried away and headed for the east hallway, certain that Ginger was staring after her. Ellen walked straight to her room, everything suddenly back in focus. The incident left her unsettled, but the rest of the day went fine, and she was embarrassed to mention it to Jake that evening.

The weekend came and Ellen found herself exhausted. "Boy, I must be getting old. I'm beat," she told Jake.

"It happens to the best of us," Jake said offhandedly. He was preoccupied, searching for something.

"Ellen, didn't you bring the mail in?"

"Yes. I thought I laid it on the desk. Did you look there?"

"I looked there and everywhere else in the house."

"Well, I know I brought it in." She joined the search, and when ten minutes of hunting hadn't produced anything, they gave up. Ellen even went back out to the mailbox to see if maybe she hadn't brought it into the house after all. Jake was irritated with her. He was Mr. Organization and they often squabbled over her haphazard ways.

Ellen went into the kitchen to start supper. She opened the refrigerator to get the lettuce for their salad, and there, on the top shelf, beaded with moisture, sat the stack of bills and letters.

"Good grief!" she shouted.

Jake came to the doorway to see what the commotion was. Ellen stood in front of the open refrigerator door sheepishly holding the droopy envelopes. "I found the mail."

"It was in the fridge?" He was incredulous. "Are you losing it, Ellen?"

She laughed, embarrassed. "I guess I'm more tired than I thought."

He shrugged his shoulders half-disgustedly, took the

mail from her, and went to the den.

That night when they were getting ready for bed, she tried to soothe his testiness by joking with him. But he turned serious.

"Are you okay, El? You've been so preoccupied lately. It's not like you to be so . . . so ding-y."

"I think I'm just tired. Work is kind of wearing on me this year for some reason."

"Okay . . ." He sounded unconvinced. "Well, get some sleep. You need it." He turned out the light, rolled over, and went to sleep himself.

Ellen lay awake a long time, mulling things over in her mind. She finally entered a fitful, restless sleep, punctuated by a bizarre dream where she was lost in a long dark hallway, and though she called and shouted, no one came to rescue her. She walked on and on down the ever narrowing passage, never finding a doorway, meeting only strangers who were as lost as she.

<hr />

The next weeks were like a nightmare. Ellen began to fear she was having a nervous breakdown. Although most days she felt perfectly in control and could almost put the disturbing incidents out of her mind, other days she felt disoriented and on edge. On those days she couldn't find any organization to her teaching. She would start a math lesson and ten minutes later she would begin it all over again. Her students, bless their hearts, took it all as a joke.

"Mrs. Brighton, you're teasing us! We just did that page."

Ellen began to fake her way through the school days. She began to avoid the other teachers because she never knew when she might say or do something stupid. She couldn't trust her own actions and reactions, and she feared her co-workers might not be as forgiving as the children were.

Jake was having a busy and frustrating year with a school bond election coming before the voters. There were meetings with the school board and public forums to preside over. Ellen had drawn into a shell, avoiding Jake. He knew something wasn't right with her, but frankly, he didn't have time to make an issue of it.

Maybe he didn't really want to face the reason why his wife could no longer balance the checkbook without his help, the reason why she asked him the same question three times in an evening; or the reason why Ellen, usually so decisive, now sometimes struggled to make the simplest decisions. When he did dare to contemplate the answers to these questions, it was easy to rationalize. Maybe this empty-nest business was having more of an effect on her than either of them had bargained for. Maybe Jerry was right, and the hormonal changes of menopause were to blame. Maybe she just had a lot on her mind. He determined to give things a few months to settle down before he confronted her.

But things didn't settle down. They got worse.

───◦◦◦◦───

Jake sat in his office on a Monday morning filling out a budget report. School was out for spring break, so no one else was in the office, but Jake was swamped with paper work and had decided to play catch-up. Ellen was shopping and wouldn't be home till after lunch.

The phone broke the silence in the empty office. He wasn't accustomed to answering his own phone, and it rang four or five times before he realized that his secretary wasn't there to get it.

"This is Jake Brighton."

"Jake . . ." It was Ellen and she was crying.

"Ellen. What's wrong? Where are you?"

"I'm at the mall. I think my car's been stolen. I've looked all over the parking lot, and it's not there." Her voice quavered.

"What? Well, where were you parked?"

"I . . . I'm not sure. I think I was in front of Penney's, but the car's not . . ." She was sobbing now. "Jake, could you just come and help me find it?"

"Where are you now, Ellen?" He was trying to be patient and not upset her any more than she already was. How could she not know where she had parked?

"I . . . I think I'm on the south side of the mall. You know—where the parking garage is. Isn't that south?"

"Yes, that's south. Are you inside?"

"Uh-huh."

"Okay. Stay right where you are, and I'll be there as soon as I can. But it'll take me at least twenty minutes to get there if I leave right now. Okay?"

Silence.

"El? Are you there?"

"I'm here."

"Are you okay?"

"Yes. Just please hurry."

"Okay. It'll be all right. Just stay there, Ellen, okay? . . . I love you."

She started crying again. "I love you too," she sobbed.

Jake locked up the office and hurried to his car. Something was terribly wrong. It wasn't like Ellen to fall apart in a situation like this. And how could she be sure the car had been stolen if she couldn't even remember where she had parked? Her memory had been terrible lately, but good grief, people didn't just completely forget where they were parked at the mall! He drove much too fast and fifteen minutes later parked illegally near the south entrance. He ran inside and stopped short just inside the door. Ellen sat on the floor under a pay phone, her hair disheveled, mascara streaking her cheeks. She looked like a derelict. Jake was almost embarrassed to claim her, but he went to her and helped her to her feet. She collapsed against him with relief. He ushered her out to his car, and the story poured out in a rush.

"I . . . I shopped all morning and then decided to get some lunch; but when I went out to the parking lot, the car was gone. At first I thought maybe I went out the wrong entrance, so I went back in and went around to the other side, but it wasn't there either. I'm so upset now, I can't remember for sure where I parked."

"Well, let's drive around and see if we can find it. Now where do you think you parked?"

"Right in front of Penney's."

Jake maneuvered through the lot and slowly drove up and down the rows in front of Penney's. In the third row, in plain sight of the entrance, sat Ellen's car.

"Ellen. There it is."

"Where?"

"Right there," he pointed.

"Where? I don't see it."

He drove over to the car and stopped directly behind it.

"What are you doing?"

"What do you mean? There's the car, right in front of you." His voice was full of disgust, and he struggled to keep from shouting at her. "I'll follow you home if you want me to. Are you done shopping?"

"I want to go home." She didn't make a move to get out

of the car. "Please . . . just take me home. I'm so mixed up."

"Ellen? What is the matter with you? You're going to have to drive the car home."

"I don't know where it is," she wailed.

He was alarmed. She was totally disoriented. This couldn't have upset her so much; something else was wrong.

He reached for her across the car's console and held her until her sobs subsided. Then he reached down beside the seat for her seat belt, buckled her in as he would a child, and turned the car toward home. They could come back for her car tonight.

Ellen was silent all the way home. She walked into the house and collapsed on the couch.

Jake went to her and sat beside her for a long time, stroking her forehead. "Honey, what is wrong? I've never seen you this upset over such a little thing."

"Jake, I'm so mixed up. I don't understand it. One minute I'm happily shopping away, and the next minute I can't even find my own car."

"Honey, I'm worried about you. I think you ought to call Jerry and make an appointment. This kind of stuff has been happening too much lately. I don't like it."

"Jake, I just had a checkup five or six months ago. I'm in perfect health. Jerry will think I'm crazy."

"Well, I'm beginning to wonder. . . ." He was half teasing, trying to lighten the moment, but Ellen was not humored.

He was afraid to leave her alone, so he worked at his desk in the den the rest of the afternoon. She puttered around the house, doing laundry, straightening her desk. By evening she was feeling cheerful, if a little embarrassed.

After supper they went back for the car, and she followed him home without incident.

Curled against Jake in their big bed, Ellen slept soundly

that night. But he woke several times, a sick feeling in his gut when he tried to fathom what all this could mean.

The next morning Jake got up early, taking care not to wake Ellen. He went into the den and dialed Jerry Morton.

"Jerry? Jake Brighton here."

"Jake, what can I do for you?"

"Well, I'm not sure. I know Ellen was in to see you a few months ago, and she said everything was fine, but something happened yesterday that has me worried." He told Dr. Morton the whole story, remembering the mail in the refrigerator and the one A.M. showers as he spoke. Jerry listened intently, and Jake wasn't comforted by his response. He sounded genuinely concerned.

"I think you'd better get her in here as soon as possible, Jake. It sounds like there's definitely something going on. I've got a pretty heavy schedule this morning, but bring her in around ten and I'll work her in. I think this is important. If for no other reason than to ease her mind."

"Okay. Thanks a lot, Jerry. I'm really sorry to bother you at home like this, but frankly, I'm pretty worried."

"Don't think a thing of it. You did the right thing to call me. I'll see you at ten."

Jake could sense that Ellen was angry that he had called Jerry without consulting her, but she showered and got dressed for the appointment without further complaint.

Jake was surprised when Dr. Morton led them to his private office rather than to an examination room. He asked each of them a barrage of questions, and the answers brought to light just how erratic Ellen's actions had been over the past months.

"Ellen, I'm just a family practice doctor, so I don't feel qualified to make any judgment calls here, but I definitely think there's something going on that needs to be looked into. I want to refer you to a specialist I know in Chicago, and then we can go from there. If you'd like me to, I can call him and set up an appointment for you. He's a neurologist . . . Dr. Patrick Muñoz."

Before Jake and Ellen left Jerry's office that morning, they had an appointment to see Dr. Muñoz on the following Wednesday morning. They spent the week in a daze—going through the motions at work and walking on eggshells at home. Ellen was sensitive and emotional; Jake, irritable and impatient.

Wednesday morning they got up at six, drove into the city, and ordered breakfast at a cafe near the medical center. They sat across from each other in a large booth, the distance widened further by their silence. They picked at their eggs and let their coffee grow cold. Finally Jake went to the counter to pay their bill, and they walked out to the parking lot and got in the car.

They arrived at Dr. Muñoz's office almost thirty minutes early and sat nervously in the waiting room, leafing blindly through ancient magazines.

Dr. Muñoz looked carefully over the charts that Jerry had sent, asked a few terse questions of his own, and before they knew what had hit them, Ellen was checked into Northwestern Memorial for what would stretch into three days of testing.

They hadn't come prepared to stay, so Jake helped Ellen get settled and then drove back to Calypso to pack a few of her things. Jake was afraid Ellen would be upset about the unexpected hospitalization, but she took the news well. In fact, Jake thought she seemed relieved to be on the brink of some answers.

Jake stayed at a hotel near the hospital on Wednesday night. He looked in on Ellen at seven A.M. and then drove back to Calypso to be at work by nine. Thursday evening after work he called Ellen. She was in good spirits and insisted that he not make the trip back into the city that night. Jake wasn't crazy about making the drive, and he had appointments scheduled in the office the next morning, so he didn't argue with her.

That evening he was bored and restless wandering around the big house. He fixed a turkey sandwich, watched the news, and decided to turn in early. But their big bed, usually so welcoming and warm, was cold and empty without Ellen. He lay awake into the early hours of the morning making deals with God.

3

Dr. Gallia's office was cold and austere, like the man who inhabited it. The receptionist pointed them toward a small alcove near the elevators, and they waited there— Ellen erect and motionless on a gray metal chair, Jake fidgeting and pacing between the window and a chair next to Ellen's. He picked up a magazine from the stack on a low table and leafed aimlessly through it, then tossed it back on the pile and resumed his pacing. It struck him that anyone watching them would have thought he was the patient.

Finally a nurse appeared in the doorway. In a soft, almost condescending voice she questioned, "Ellen Brighton?"

Ellen looked up, obviously recognizing her name, but didn't move from her seat. Jake nodded to the nurse and took Ellen's arm and led her, following the nurse down the sterile hall. The pungent odor of alcohol and disinfectant assaulted Jake's nostrils. Once he would have perceived the odor as clean, even wholesome. Now it repulsed him, conjuring images of death and decay.

The nurse motioned for Ellen to take a seat on the side of the examining table. Jake felt awkward and irrelevant, towering as he did over both women. He took a seat on the rolling stool at the foot of the table and then realized that this was the doctor's seat. Finally, he settled on a folding chair that had been hidden behind the open door.

Ellen had not spoken since they got off the elevator, and Jake wondered what she was thinking. The thoughts she had given voice to lately were so inscrutable that some days he despaired of ever understanding her mind again.

He had tried to talk to her about the problems she was having. He knew she must be worried too. They had always been able to talk things out with each other in the past. But whenever he questioned her now—and he was always gentle about it—she would pretend that she hadn't heard him, or would change the subject. Or she would give him a quasi-reply that had almost nothing to do with what he had asked.

The nurse took Ellen's blood pressure, pulse, and temperature, recording them on her chart in silence. Then without explanation or instruction, she left the room. Jake was becoming frustrated with the sterility of not only the premises, but the personnel, as well. How out of place a warm smile would have been in this frigid clinic—but how welcome!

Three days of testing at Northwestern Memorial had produced nothing definite. They had waited an endless two weeks for the test results, and now Dr. Muñoz had sent them to Dr. William Gallia, one of the many doctors in the hospital with whom they had consulted. He had a reputation for being one of Chicago's finest neurologists, but Jake felt his talents must lie in an area other than patient-physician rapport. He struck Jake as aloof and uncaring. Now they sat in this joyless room waiting for him to sentence her—or acquit her.

Finally after twenty minutes, Dr. Gallia tapped on the door and entered before either of them could respond. He was shorter than Jake remembered from their first meeting, with a fringe of white hair emphasizing the shiny baldness of his head. He wore wire-framed glasses low on his nose and looked over these as he addressed Ellen.

"Hello, Mrs. Brighton. How are you feeling today?"

Ellen spoke slowly, suspiciously. "I'm fine, I guess. I wish you would all figure out what's wrong with me so I can get on with life." She didn't sound like herself, and Jake wanted to apologize for her. Compared to her usual friendly way, she seemed almost rude. But these people didn't know her, so he kept silent. Ellen had retreated to that place deep inside her mind where it seemed she fled so often recently.

The doctor looked at Ellen's chart in his hands, appearing to avoid her eyes as he spoke. "Well, for starters I'm going to have you answer a few questions for the nurse. If you'll go with her to the conference room across the hall, your husband and I will join you in just a few minutes."

Jake wasn't fooled for a minute by this ruse, but Ellen seemed not to think anything was amiss. Still fully clothed, she slid off the side of the examining table and, giving Jake a backward glance, followed the nurse out the door.

Dr. Gallia wasted no time coming to the point.

"Mr. Brighton, I see from your wife's records that she has completed a battery of tests at the medical center?" He spoke it like a question but didn't pause for a response. "I'm very sorry to have to be the bearer of bad news, but it appears that your wife has a disease called Alzheimer's. Are you familiar with the term?"

Jake nodded, stunned. Though he heard the doctor's next words clearly, they came as through a long tunnel, muffled and echoing back at him.

"I must say that it is rather unusual, though not unheard

of, to see this in someone as young as your wife. Unfortunately, we are beginning to see Alzheimer's more and more in people in their forties and fifties. You must understand that there isn't a definitive test for Alzheimer's, except with an autopsy, but I'm making as positive a diagnosis as I can. With this disease we rely a lot on the process of elimination. The tests your wife went through rule out the other disorders we might suspect with her symptoms"—he counted them off on his fingers—"Parkinson's, Multi-infarct dementia, Pick's Disease . . ."

Jake had been doing his own research, and these names were familiar to him. For each new disease he had read about, he found a paragraph that seemed to describe Ellen's symptoms perfectly. But now he had a name—a label to put on all this craziness—*Alzheimer's*.

Dr. Gallia continued. "We can't detect any evidence of a stroke or hormone imbalance. Of course, as I said, Alzheimer's cannot be confirmed except by autopsy, but the tests she took pretty much exclude any other possibilities. I think we're looking at a classic case of Alzheimer's here, with the only variable being the early onset."

Jake watched the doctor in a state of shock, detached from the scene . . . everything seemed to be in slow motion. Dr. Gallia took off his glasses, rubbed the bridge of his nose, and sat with his head bent for so long Jake began to wonder if he was fighting his emotions or if he had gone to sleep. But when the doctor looked up, his expression was matter-of-fact. He picked up a prescription pad and began writing as he spoke.

"I'm going to refer you to the Alzheimer's Association. It is an excellent national organization that was started right here in Chicago. They can recommend some books and other literature that will be helpful. They also have a number of support groups in this area. At some point I think you will find it very helpful to speak with others who are going through the same things you will be."

Jake was numb. The color drained from his face, and he felt his heart begin to beat erratically in his chest. He managed to blurt out a few rudimentary questions.

"Where . . . where do we go from here? Isn't there some sort of medicine or therapy or something we can do?"

Dr. Gallia sighed deeply, the first sign of humaneness he had exhibited. "Mr. Brighton, what you can do is take your wife home and enjoy the next days and weeks and months as much as possible. Try to keep life as normal and routine as possible. Above all, don't fall into the trap of treating her like an invalid. There will be plenty of time for that later. See to it that she does everything she can possibly do for herself for as long as she can. It may be helpful to seek counseling for both your wife and yourself, for this is a very difficult disease to deal with. Certainly if you want to try some physical therapy or speech therapy when the time comes, you have every right to do that; but my personal opinion is that those things are basically a waste of valuable time."

He paused to let his words sink in. "I won't lie to you, Mr. Brighton. This is not a pretty disease. You must accept the fact that over the next few years your wife is going to change drastically. Of course, we can't predict how quickly the disease will progress. It varies greatly from one person to the next."

The truth slowly began to register. Jake stumbled to his feet and stood behind his chair, clutching its back for support. "But isn't there some sort of drug you can give her . . . there's surely some kind of medicine for this? There must be something!"

Jake began to pace back and forth in the tiny space in front of the doctor's desk. Panic rose in his throat. His hands grasped at the empty air as though he could pull an answer from its nothingness.

He was met with Dr. Gallia's calm, clinical reply. "At some point we will probably prescribe tranquilizers or possibly an antidepressant, depending on the direction the disease takes with your wife. There are a few experimental drugs in the works, but as far as a wonder drug, I'm sorry, there just isn't anything."

Jake abruptly stopped pacing. "What . . . what caused this? Why Ellen?"

"We don't know. Some studies seem to indicate . . ."

But Jake wasn't listening. His mind was racing, and he interrupted as a new thought pounded into his brain. "Is this . . . is it terminal?"

"Alzheimer's causes actual disintegration of the tissues of the brain, so yes, in that sense it is terminal. And there is no cure. Of course, as I said, every case is different, so I don't ever put a time frame on it; but generally we see patients surviving anywhere from five to fifteen years, possibly a bit longer, though frankly, that is no blessing. When early onset is a factor, frequently the survival time is shorter. It's often infections—pneumonia and such—that cause death in these patients, especially after they have become bedridden."

Dr. Gallia stood, dismissing Jake. "I know I've given you a great deal to think about, Mr. Brighton. Please get in touch with the Alzheimer's Association. They will be very helpful in answering your questions . . . and you'll have many questions."

"How . . . how soon should we come back for an appointment?" Jake was grasping at straws. He wasn't ready to be dismissed. He wasn't ready to deal with this yet. How could he face Ellen with such devastating news?

"I don't see any reason why your own physician can't

handle things from here. Unless she gets sick, there's really no reason for her to see a doctor other than for regular checkups. Of course, if she begins to decline rapidly, or you feel she would benefit from antidepressant medication or sedatives, then you may want to have her reevaluated."

Jake slammed his fist into the palm of his other hand, wishing it were a wall. *Gets sick?* Good grief! What was wrong with this man? Couldn't he see that she *was* sick? How could he calmly sit here and tell him that his Ellen— his sweet, beautiful Ellen—was going to die a slow, horrible death . . . was going to rot away? And there wasn't a blessed thing he could do about it.

His anger threatened to explode in physical violence. He clasped his hands in front of him and willed himself to calm down. He had to face Ellen, and he couldn't do it in anger.

He took a deep breath to compose himself, and nodding to the doctor he left the room, closing the door behind him.

Ellen was waiting for him in the alcove. She stood and met him by the elevator, and they rode to the lobby in silence. So much silence between them now. It nearly killed Jake.

He drove home while she dozed in the front seat beside him. His mind was churning with thoughts of what the future might hold for them. He tried to will the awful visions away, but it was like a physical battle. He was drenched in sweat, his breath coming in short gasps.

He watched her face as she slept beside him, unable to fathom that inside the beautiful head that lay on his shoulder each night—the head he cradled so tenderly—a vile thing was eating away at her brain. It was incomprehensible. It had to be a bad dream. Surely he would wake up, and they would laugh together about it as they had often laughed about other silly dreams.

Ellen instinctively woke up as they pulled into their

driveway. They carried the paraphernalia of the day's trip into the kitchen. Ellen still had not spoken a word. She puttered around the house, hanging up jackets, putting receipts in the desk drawer. She went to the sink and began washing the few dishes they had left there from breakfast. Jake watched her perform these mundane chores with new eyes. How long would she be able to do these simple, homely things? Suddenly he was overwhelmed with love and tenderness for this woman—his wife. He went to her as she stood at the sink and wrapped his arms around her, resting his chin on the top of her head. Her hair was disheveled from sleeping in the car, and her skin was damp from the steam of the dishwater. She turned to him, put her arms around his waist, and laid her head on his chest, uttering two simple words: "Tell me."

Jake fought to control his emotions. "It's Alzheimer's, Ellen. At least it's not any of the other things they tested you for, so they think that's what it has to be."

Calmly, as though it were a relief to finally have a name for this intruder, she sighed. "I thought so. I thought that's what you were going to tell me." Ellen had been researching too. Jake knew that she had tried not to look very far into her future, but words like senility and dementia and, yes, even Alzheimer's, must have danced disturbingly through her mind in the past weeks and months.

Her voice sounded strangely serene. "Jake. How long do I have?"

"They don't know. They just know that things will get worse." He couldn't bring himself to tell her five years.

She began to cry. With tears streaming down her face and with quivering voice, she wailed, "Oh, Jake! I'm so sorry. I didn't want it to happen this way. I always pictured us growing old together . . . enjoying our grandchildren . . . and great-grandchildren. Oh, how will we tell the kids. . . ?

But then, I guess they know something's wrong with me as crazy as I've been acting lately. It's funny, but it's kind of nice to know I'm not losing my marbles . . . well, I guess I am, but at least I have an excuse." She laughed through her tears.

She was more lucid than Jake had seen her in weeks. He felt an urgent need to tell her all the things he loved about her. How do you tell someone that they are life itself to you? How do you say goodbye when there is no leave-taking? But they might not have another time to say goodbye. There might not be another day when she would grasp his words of love. And so he ventured to speak what was beyond words.

He led her to the darkened living room and laid a fire in the fireplace while she watched in silence. She sat down on the sofa, but Jake sat on the floor in front of the hearth and pulled her into his lap.

"Ellen . . ." His voice faltered. He stroked her temple and traced the lines that so many years of smiles had etched on her face. "Ellen, I love you with all my heart. I never knew that a man could be so happy and so utterly content until I met you. Do you know how happy you make me, El? You mean everything to me . . . everything."

He stopped, not trusting his voice. Then feeling an urgency to spill everything that was in his heart, he went on. "I don't know what this is we're facing now, but if it means losing you I'm not sure how I'll go on. Whatever happens, El, I don't want you to be afraid of anything. No matter how awful it might get, I'll be here for you. We'll . . ." He started to say, "We'll beat this thing," but he knew better, and he knew that she knew better. He wanted to keep things honest between them. They had never had secrets from each other.

"We'll get through this somehow," he said finally.

"Oh, Jake, if I died tomorrow I'd have no regrets."

Her voice was beautiful in his ear—low and husky and familiar.

"But . . . I'm afraid of living beyond tomorrow . . . that I'm going to be a burden to you and the kids. Oh, Jake, I love you. I love you so much . . . so very much. And I know with all my heart that you love me, but I'm terrified our love won't survive this . . . this monster! I feel . . . possessed! I've never felt out of control like this before, and it terrifies me . . . Oh, Jake, I'm so scared."

They held each other, praying together, drawing strength and comfort from the physical embrace and from the presence of the God they knew and trusted, even though they didn't understand what was happening to them.

As the fire waned, their embrace turned to passion. They drank each other in, making love unhurriedly, but with fervid insistence . . . with sweet familiarity.

Afterward, Jake brought a quilt and pillows from their bed. He stoked the fire, and they slept on the floor in front of the hearth until the harsh light of morning flooded their makeshift bed, and the embers grew as cold as the reality they woke to face.

4

Dr. Gallia's words were prophetic. As the months passed, Jake watched Ellen fade before his eyes. The memory losses became more frequent and more glaring.

Ellen loved to cook, but now she could no longer remember the simple recipes she had made from scratch since she was a young girl on the farm.

She went completely blank when trying to tell Jake about a phone call. She knew someone had called, and that it was important, but she couldn't remember what it was about, or whether it was a man or a woman she had spoken to. She tried writing down phone messages, but too often the jumbled scribblings on the notepad gave neither her nor Jake a clue about the call. Jake finally bought an answering machine, but Ellen would hurry to answer the phone before the machine could pick up the call. "What if it's you, Jake? Or one of the kids?" she reasoned. He couldn't make her understand that she could listen to the message and then pick up the phone. It was all too confusing and complicated for her.

Sometimes the names of even her closest friends escaped her, and though she could usually conjure them up within the course of the call, increasingly her conversations became erratic and bizarre.

Almost comically, Jake began to find things in the strangest places. A pencil in the toothbrush holder, a slice of toast in the desk drawer by the telephone, and a stick of butter—thankfully still in its wrapper—in his underwear drawer. He had to laugh at that one. Even Ellen had seen the humor in it, though she was angry when she heard him laughingly tell Brant about it on the phone.

They hadn't yet told the kids about the diagnosis. Ellen wasn't ready to admit the truth to her children. Jake had to respect her wishes, but he knew that they were worried and puzzled by the changes they saw in their mother, for they had caught her in some of her silly mistakes. Subtly, he tried to prepare them for the news by dropping little hints about her confusion.

There were brief intermissions, sometimes lasting for days, when Ellen seemed to be her old self. And during those times, Jake found himself hoping that it had all been a mistake. Maybe the doctors were wrong. Maybe it was really something else, and she was getting well. It amazed him that he could be so devastated when he saw the symptoms return. It was like finding out about the Alzheimer's all over again. He almost wished the remissions wouldn't occur, because the telltale warnings always came back, and when they came back they were worse than before.

Sometimes she just lost words. She would be talking along making perfect sense, when suddenly she would stop in midsentence, unable to think of the next word she wanted to say. Sometimes Jake could supply it for her. They had always finished each other's sentences. But more and more she lost words that he couldn't find for her. She became agitated when he reeled off a multiple-choice list. The answer was often "none of the above." Occasionally she could dredge up the word if he was patient and allowed her to concentrate, but usually she waved him away, leaving the thought unfinished and both of them feeling frustrated.

More disturbing, Jake noticed that she had begun to use completely nonsensical words. Sometimes she was aware that what she said hadn't made a whit of sense, and she could backtrack and find the right word, the right phrase. But most of the time she seemed unaware that she had said anything amiss. If it hadn't been so tragic, it might have been comical.

One night while she and Jake were watching TV in the den, she turned to him and said incredulously, "I don't see why these donney on the brackers!"

"What?" Jake asked, looking at her askance.

She sighed and slowly articulated, as though speaking to a half-wit, "I don't see why these donney on the brackers!"

"Ellen, I don't have the faintest idea what you are saying."

She laughed and shook her head like a dog shaking dry after a bath. "Well, I don't either, Jake." Ellen started giggling. It was a contagious, bubbling laughter, and Jake began to laugh with her. They laughed till they were holding their bellies and wiping away tears. Then abruptly Ellen's face contorted, and her guffaws became sobs—maniacal, bellowing sobs. She was nearly hysterical and inconsolable. Jake tried to put his arms around her, but she shoved him away with a strength that surprised them both.

She sat on the sofa hugging her knees to her chin, rocking back and forth, sobbing.

Jake felt like a spineless coward, but he couldn't stay in the room with her another minute. He backed away, grabbed his jacket off the hook in the front hall, and fled into the chilly night.

The street was dark and a light mist dampened the pavement so that the streetlights were multiplied in the reflection. Jake jogged briskly for a few minutes. Then, out of breath, he slowed to a walk.

The streets were deserted, but Jake was acutely, painfully aware of the lights that burned in the windows of the large homes that lined either side of the street. Here and there he could hear music floating from an open door. And through curtains, not yet closed to the evening darkness, he saw life going on as usual for those within. Businessmen read newspapers in their easy chairs; children argued over games; mothers rocked their babies. Their world—his and Ellen's—was falling in upon them, yet all around them life went on.

Jake felt despair creep over him like a vine. What would become of them? Communication had always been the foundation of their marriage. They had taken immense joy in discussing people, politics, philosophy, psychology. And if an exchange turned into a debate or even an argument, so much the better. They had never been happier than when they wrangled over some controversial topic. It had become a high for them, an energizer. With their words, they had played an exhilarating game of catch—tossing ideas and waiting with anticipation for them to be thrown back. Now he threw words against a hard wall, and if they came back to him at all, they came back senseless and unpredictable.

There were so many things they could have gone without—their wealth, their sight, their arms or legs. *Why?* Jake railed. Why did it have to be their words? And it was *their* words, for Ellen's silences left him as impotent of speech as if he physically shared her disease.

Suddenly Jake was filled with rage. He shook his fist at

the heavens, and through clenched teeth he shouted into the darkness, not caring who heard. "Why, God? Tell me *why*!" But the heavens were as a canyon. His voice echoed back to him through the empty street—the only answer the gentle sound of the rain on the pavement.

He sat down on the curb, utterly exhausted. The rain had soaked into his jeans, leaving him shivering and damp. Hopelessness seeped into every fiber of his being, and for the first time since little Catherine had died, he put his head in his hands and sobbed.

He cried till there were no tears left. Then he picked himself up leadenly and walked slowly back to the house. The lights were off downstairs, but the lamp in their attic bedroom still burned.

Ellen was sitting up in bed, pretending to read, when she heard Jake come up the stairs. He came quietly into the room, and she could see that he was upset and exhausted.

He looked at her and shrugged, and she knew that he simply didn't know what to say to her.

She started to cry. "Oh, Jake. Please. Please don't look at me that way. I don't want to be this way . . . can't you see? I want what we had before. I want my . . . my life back. I want . . . I want . . . oh, I don't even know what to say . . . how to say it. I don't even know. . . ." She gave him a look of sorrowful apology. "I'm losing my mind, Jake. I feel like I'm losing my mind," she said with resignation.

He went to her wordlessly and sat down beside her on the bed. He wrapped his arms around her and pulled her into his embrace, leaning back against the headboard with her in his arms.

They lay that way until gently, wordlessly, Jake got up from the bed. He kissed Ellen and pulled the covers around her, tucking her in like a child. Then he went into the bathroom, and Ellen heard the comforting sound of water splashing in the sink as her husband performed his nightly ritual of brushing his teeth and washing his face.

∞

The most difficult thing for Ellen was telling the kids.

"I don't want them to worry about me," she told Jake. And then, her voice tinged with anger, she added, "And I don't want to spend the rest of my life having them watching me . . . just waiting for me to do something stupid—just waiting for me to go crazy."

Jake had agreed to hold off as long as they could, but in the nine months since Ellen had been diagnosed, her children were frighteningly aware that something was wrong and had been for a long time.

Jake wanted to get things out in the open and get it over with, but Ellen begged him to wait till the end of Christmas vacation before they broke the awful news.

The first few days the boys were home, Ellen was withdrawn and irritable. Jake made a wide berth for her by keeping Brant and Kyle occupied decorating for Christmas.

It was a Brighton tradition—since they had moved into the big house—to outline the roof, doors, and windows with white lights. Perched precariously on the roof, they were grateful for the warmer-than-usual December weather and the absence of ice or snow. It was late in the season to be putting lights up, but Jake couldn't bear to not put them up at all. He had waited until the boys were home to help him; he certainly didn't want Ellen on the roof. When the lights were in place, they put the tree up in the living room and hung five stockings on the mantel. Ellen shouted suggestions from the kitchen but left the decorating to them.

The rest of their time was spent playing basketball at the

high school gym and watching football on TV.

Jana and Mark came from Chicago two days before Christmas. Howard and MaryEllen were arriving on Christmas Eve, and everyone assumed they would have the traditional turkey dinner they'd been having for years. They were accustomed to Ellen taking charge, especially in the kitchen; but so far she had made no effort toward planning or preparing the meal. Finally Jake made a list and went with Ellen to the grocery store. He bought cranberries for the sauce he was sure she could no longer remember how to make. Maybe MaryEllen would get there in time to prepare it. It didn't matter anymore, really.

They finished their shopping, and Jake carried the groceries into the kitchen, setting the heavy bags on the countertop. Ellen made no move to put things away, so Jake enlisted Mark and Jana to do the job while he hunted the recipes and assembled the ingredients for the dishes that needed to be started early.

Jake saw Jana try to catch his eye, but he looked away and pretended not to see her questioning glances. It was so unusual for him to be supervising the kitchen. He knew Jana was confused and worried.

"Are you feeling okay, Mom?" Jana asked tentatively.

"I'm just fine."

"Are you sure? You look tired."

"I'm fine." Ellen's terse reply only served to worry Jana more.

For the rest of the afternoon Ellen hovered in the kitchen, but she was content to let Jana and Jake do most of the cooking and cleaning up. She was in their way, and she was cranky and short with both of them. Jake could see that Jana's feelings were hurt.

He discovered Jana in tears in the downstairs bedroom that had been hers as a teenager, and he knew then that they couldn't wait another minute to get things out in the open. He pleaded with Ellen to let him call the kids together and tell them. But she argued almost viciously with him.

"Jake, I don't want to ruin everybody's Christmas," she snarled between clenched teeth.

"El, everybody's Christmas is already being ruined by the way you are acting. You're just putting off the inevitable. Either you tell them or I will." He knew it was cruel, but it was the truth, and she needed to hear it. Uncharacteristically she sulked. Finally she acquiesced, and Jake called them all into the living room that evening after supper. With Ellen at his side, silent and embarrassed, he disclosed everything the doctors had told them.

"I know you kids are aware that something has been going on here for a while that we haven't let you in on. I'm sorry for the worry it has caused you, but we . . . Mom . . . didn't want to worry you any sooner than we had to. We're not ready to tell this to anyone else, but . . . well, it's time you know the truth. We'll tell Grandma and Grandpa tomorrow."

Oh, how he hated to have to be telling his precious children this news! At this moment he suddenly understood more clearly the reservations Ellen had about revealing her illness. He paused and sighed heavily. "Kids, we found out a few months ago that the doctors think Mom has Alzheimer's Disease. You know what that is, don't you?"

Kyle was hesitant. "Alzheimer's? I thought . . . I thought that was like being senile . . . like old people get."

"It is, kind of, Kyle. Except you don't necessarily have to be old to have Alzheimer's." He went on then to explain everything they had learned over the past months. It was a tearful meeting, and Jake knew from experience that it would take a while for the import of what he had told them to soak in. He and Ellen were just beginning to accept what was happening to them, and they'd had months to get used to the idea.

It turned out to be a week of special closeness for the family. Jake and Ellen together told her parents the next day, and while Howard and MaryEllen were stunned, they too had known that something was wrong. They were strong for Ellen's sake, and she was comforted by their presence and relieved to have at least the burden of secrecy lifted.

The kids were refreshingly open and candid about everything. The next day Jana went straight to the library and checked out a stack of books on Alzheimer's. She brought them home and plopped them ceremoniously in the middle of the dining room table. All evening long, she and the boys pored over them, reading paragraphs aloud and grilling their parents about the symptoms Ellen had experienced so far.

They were like detectives hot on the trail of solving a mystery. They were even able to find humor in the sorrow, teasing Ellen affectionately.

Jake knew, though, that they had their moments of private anguish. Kyle, especially, seemed to be in denial. He would read about a particular symptom and say, "You've never done that, Mom. Maybe the doctors are wrong. All these books say they really can't know for sure if it's Alzheimer's."

"Honey, I have done that. Just ask Dad."

Jake would confirm it, and Kyle would go to the books again, looking for nonexistent proof that this was all a horrible mistake.

Ellen saw the pain that darkened Kyle's eyes and longed to see a glimpse of the carefree, mischievous boy who had brightened this house so many months ago. But the boy was becoming a man. Ellen's heart ached for him. *Oh, this boy . . . this boy of mine. He's trying so hard. Why do I have to hurt him like this? Why? My little boy. Sometimes I can't even re-member his name. But I know he's mine . . . my little boy and he's trying so hard . . . so hard.* The thoughts roiled disjoint-edly in her mind.

The day before the boys were to leave to go back to school, Ellen looked out the living room window onto the wide driveway. Kyle was on the concrete, wearing only shorts and a sweatshirt in spite of the cold. He stood under the basketball hoop that Jake had erected when the boys were just learning to play. He was smashing the ball into the net, hooking the rebound and smashing it up again with all his strength. From his reddened face and his clenched jaw, Ellen knew he was furious. She started out the door and then thought better of it. *Let him get it out of his system. Maybe this is his way of working out his anger.*

Kyle came in an hour later with a new peace about him. He was so sweet with Ellen that it made her heart ache. But the sweetness was also a healing balm for her spirit.

When the boys pulled out of the driveway that last Sun-day night, Ellen was no less forgetful, her words no less jum-bled, her actions no less awkward. But her son's love had transformed her. Tranquility shone on her face and a re-newed sense of self-worth buoyed her spirit.

⸺⸺∞⸺⸺

On an unseasonably warm Saturday evening in Febru-ary, Ellen had invited her closest friend to have dinner with them. Ellen and Sandra had been friends since they had taught together during Ellen's first year at Calypso Elemen-tary.

Sandra Brenner's husband had left her after six years of marriage, leaving her with two small daughters to raise. Her girls were grown and married now. One a lawyer and the other a nurse, they were a walking testimony to the sacrifices their mother had made for them. Sandra had made the best of a difficult situation. Jake had always admired the courage and tenacity that were so incongruous to her petite, pixielike appearance. She was frank, and she could be brash, but those qualities had served her well. Jake couldn't help liking her.

He was turning burgers on the grill in the backyard when Sandra came out on the deck. Jake could see Ellen through the kitchen windows chopping vegetables for a salad. Sandra didn't mince words.

"Jake, what's going on with Ellen?"

He hesitated. "What do you mean?"

"Hey, if it's none of my business, just say so, but don't try to act like everything is hunky-dory when we both know it's not."

Jake looked through the window and saw that Ellen was still at the counter. He let out his breath.

"Sandra, she's not ready to talk about it. It would be better for everybody if she would talk to you." He paused, trying to decide what to say next. "Listen, I know you have a pretty good idea what's going on, but, Sandra, I can't breach her trust. The details will have to come from her. Have you asked her about it?"

"I've hinted. She's not taking the bait."

He gave her a laconic smile. "It's not like you to just hint around . . . I don't know what to say, Sandra . . . it's not my decision to make. But I think if you just come out and ask her, she might be willing to talk to you."

"Yeah, if she can remember who I am." Her tone was caustic, sarcastic, but her voice trailed off when she heard the door slam and saw Ellen come onto the deck.

"Are the . . . the . . . hamburgers . . . hamburgers almost done, Jake? Everything's ready in the kitchen." Ellen was in a cheerful mood, oblivious to the conversation she had interrupted.

Jake shrugged behind Ellen's back and gave Sandra a "what can I say" look. He followed the women into the kitchen.

Dinner was a disaster. Ellen had salted and peppered the salad until it was inedible. The first bite nearly choked Jake, but he just pushed it aside without comment. Sandra was saved from the salad when Ellen knocked her Coke over, sending a stream of the dark, fizzing liquid onto the floor. This type of thing was happening more and more frequently. The doctors had told them that Ellen would eventually lose her muscle coordination, but Jake thought it was more a matter of just forgetting where she had set things. Usually Jake just cleaned things up, and they tried to pretend it hadn't happened. In front of Sandra, the humiliation was beyond ignoring. Ellen burst into tears and ran from the room.

Jake wiped at the sticky puddle under the table with a kitchen towel and motioned for Sandra to go to Ellen.

Sandra found Ellen huddled on the floor of the bathroom, mindlessly blotting at a dark stain on her blouse with the damp washcloth clutched in her fist. She knelt down beside Ellen and put her arm around her.

"What is it, Ellen? Please tell me."

Ellen looked up, her face a mask of despair. "I can't even feed myself anymore, Sandra."

"Ellen, what is it?" Sandra repeated.

"It's . . . I have Alzheimer's," she choked. "Oh, Sandra, I'm going crazy!" It was almost a scream.

As she comprehended the truth of Ellen's words—a truth she had suspected all along—tears of sorrow streamed down her own face. Sandra wrapped her arms around her friend. "Oh, Ellen," she said simply.

Ellen's voice rose hysterically, and her words came out in agonized sobs. "Oh, Sandra, how can Jake stand me like this? How long can he put up with this? I need him, Sandra. I need him. I love him."

Now she turned her diatribe heavenward. She shook her fists and raged, "God! Help me. I need help. God? Don't do this to me. Where are you? Where? Where?"

For an hour they sat side by side on the cold tile floor. Sandra let Ellen pour out all her secret fears, all her rage. And when Ellen had seemingly been drained of every word, they stood and went together to tell Jake that Sandra knew everything.

It was a relief to Jake to have someone else to share this horrible secret. Now that Ellen had confided her fears in Sandra, some of the pressure was off him. He was guiltily grateful.

⬳⬳⬳

Shortly after ten one night a few weeks later, the phone rang. Jake was in the den watching the late news. Ellen had gone to bed half an hour before, claiming exhaustion, so Jake hurried to answer the phone before the extension in their room woke her.

"Jake?"

"Yes?"

"Jake, hi. This is Carolyn Linmeyer." Carolyn was the principal at Calypso Elementary. "Is Ellen there?"

"Well, yes, but she's gone to bed. I can wake her if you need to talk to her."

Carolyn cleared her throat and sounded nervous as she continued. "No, no. Actually, it's you I need to talk to. I just . . . well, I wanted to make sure Ellen wasn't standing right there."

Jake's palms went clammy, and he felt the adrenaline begin to flow. He was terrified of what he knew Carolyn was going to say next.

"Jake, this is really difficult for me. I'm not sure how to put this, but . . . Ellen has been having some real problems at school." There was a long pause on Carolyn's end, and Jake didn't know how to respond.

Finally, feeling cruel for putting the burden on her, but not knowing what else to say, he asked, "Exactly what kind of problems, Carolyn?"

"Well, frankly, Jake, I'm worried about Ellen. She seems like she's under a lot of pressure lately. I don't know how to describe it, but she just isn't herself. I don't want to alarm you, but . . . she's done some really . . . well, strange things the last few weeks. I know this sounds crazy, but she's gotten lost in the hallways at school—more than once, Jake. She's done things like forget to send her class down to lunch. And . . . and one day in a staff meeting she just blanked out when I asked her a question. It was like she didn't even hear me. She just looked at me, even after I repeated the question. It was very uncomfortable, and some of the other teachers questioned me about it later. I'm not sure Ellen was even aware of what happened." Carolyn's voice picked up steam as she recited the litany of Ellen's violations, obviously not wanting to chicken out before she had said it all. Now she caught her breath and, almost contritely, added, "I hope I'm not out of line, Jake, but we're all very concerned about her. And it seems to be getting worse. I . . . I just felt like you needed to know."

Jake struggled with what to say next. He had put Carolyn in an awful position. She had been forced to tell her boss that his wife was incompetent. He and Ellen had agreed they would not tell anyone about the diagnosis until it was absolutely necessary. It seemed that time had now come, but Jake felt like a traitor.

He took a deep breath and plunged in. "Carolyn, I'm sorry this has put you in such an uncomfortable position. I'd like this to stay completely confidential until Ellen and I can discuss it, but I feel you deserve to know what's going on here." He paused, trying to decide where to begin. "Do you remember last March when Ellen took those three days of leave?"

"Yes." There was curiosity and concern in Carolyn's voice.

"Well, Ellen had been having some problems with her memory, some problems sleeping . . . some other symptoms. Our doctor sent her to a specialist, and she was put through some pretty extensive testing. She was in the hospital those three days . . . and what they came up with was . . . well, they think Ellen has Alzheimer's Disease."

"Oh, Jake! Oh no. I can't believe it. Oh, I'm so sorry . . . but . . . she's so young!"

"I know. It usually doesn't strike people Ellen's age, but that's what they think we're dealing with. I know we should have told you sooner, Carolyn. It wasn't right to make you deal with this. Things have been pretty bad here at home, too, so it was foolish of me to think they'd be any better there. I . . . I guess I haven't wanted to admit just how serious this is getting. I'm so sorry, Carolyn. I'm sorry this has fallen on you. But, well, Ellen didn't want to tell people yet. We're . . . we're struggling to keep things as normal as possible."

"Oh, I understand. Oh, Jake, I can't tell you how sorry I am. This is really terrible."

"It's been pretty devastating." Then and there, he made a decision. It seemed so strange for him to be making plans that would change Ellen's life forever, without even discussing it with her. "This is going to be very difficult for

Ellen, but I think it would be best for everyone concerned if we get a substitute for her the rest of the week and start looking for a replacement immediately. I would feel terrible if . . . well, if anything happened."

Carolyn started to protest, but Jake spared her the half-hearted attempts. They both knew there were no other options.

"We need to be very sensitive how we present this to Ellen's class. It won't be easy to explain to second graders. I'll trust you to handle that, Carolyn. Maybe we can buy some time with the substitute and wait until next week to tell everyone. That'll give me a chance to break the decision gently to Ellen."

"Okay."

"I appreciate your concern, Carolyn. I know it wasn't easy for you to call me. I shouldn't have let it go so long."

"I don't know what to say . . . I'm still shocked by this news. But please . . . please know that we'll be praying for you, Jake."

"Thank you, Carolyn." He was touched and his voice broke. "That means a lot to me."

Jake put the receiver gently in the cradle and sat at the desk, unmoving. From the den, the sound of the TV sportscaster droned on and on, the volume barely audible.

How could he have let this go on? He had put Ellen's coworkers in an awful position. He had forced Carolyn to make this difficult phone call, had possibly even put children in danger. Was he blind? Couldn't he see that Ellen was long past the stage of being able to do her job? He would never have forgiven himself if he had allowed a tragedy to happen because of his misjudgment. He had put his own job in jeopardy with his foolish . . . was it denial? Is this what denial was like? He'd been blind!

Finally Jake got up, switched off the TV, and climbed the

stairs to their attic bedroom. His feet were like lead, and he felt a hundred years old. He tried to pray. He knew he needed strength that he didn't possess, but his lips could form only one word—*please*.

Ellen lay curled up in bed, clutching the blankets under her chin. Even in sleep her fists were clenched, and her face wore an expression that was almost a grimace. There was no peace for her even in her dreams. Jake watched her chest rise and fall under the layers of quilts. And he wished he could crawl into bed beside her and never wake up.

—∞∞—

Ellen cried when Jake told her about Carolyn's phone call the next morning. She saw in his eyes that it killed him to have to reveal to her the humiliating things that were being said about her at school. But in a moment of clarity, she also realized that she would never have accepted his gentle ultimatum—that she simply could not teach any longer—if he had not given her the stark truth. Ellen had always been a strong woman, and she wasn't used to having Jake make decisions for her. A year ago she would have argued with him—maybe even defied him and gone to work anyway. But now she could only cry.

How many more things would be taken away from her before this was all over? She was just beginning to grasp the reality that her future had been stolen from her. Now her present had been taken as well.

Slowly, with sorrowful reluctance, she was letting go of her dreams of watching her children grow and marry, of enjoying the grandchildren they would have given her. She had said goodbye to the dreams she and Jake had shared of traveling together.

Now she needed to tell Jake goodbye, as well. The single

redeeming thing she had discovered in the chasm of this disease was that she had been given an opportunity that most deaths did not allow. She had been given a chance to say goodbye, to voice all the things that death sometimes left unsaid. As she felt herself gripped ever more tightly by the claws of dementia, she began to feel panicked that she might let that opportunity slip away; that she would be swallowed by the abyss before she had declared her love for Jake—her precious Jake.

Somehow, today, seeing Jake vulnerable and broken as he gave her the news about Carolyn's call, Ellen knew it was time.

She reached for him from her place in the bed, where he had awakened her to tell her the hurtful news. He sat down beside her, and she leaned her head against his chest. In words that she realized were neither eloquent nor precise, she spoke of her love for him, her sorrow for what they were losing.

"Jake . . . Jake. Oh, how I've loved you. I . . . I'm so sorry for this. I'm so sorry to . . . to . . ." In her mind the word "disappoint" was sharp and clear, but she could not get it to form on her lips. She let it drop and struggled to go on. "You've been so good, Jake. So good to me . . . to the kids. I . . . I can't believe this is happening to us . . . I can't . . ." She started to cry softly.

Jake stroked her cheek and tried to quiet her with gentle murmurs of "Shh. Shh. Shh."

"No, Jake. Don't hush me. I want to tell you. I want to love you. I want . . . I want . . ." She felt the familiar fog of confusion begin to creep up on her, and desperately she struggled to finish her thought. "Please, Jake. Don't forget me. Don't let the kids forget me. Please, Jake, will you tell my grandchildren about me . . . tell them how much I would have loved them."

Jake squeezed her so tightly she winced in pain. His voice in her ear was gravelly with emotion. "Ellen, how could I ever forget you? You're the love of my life. Don't you know that, honey? I'll never forget you," he whispered.

"I do know it . . . I do . . ." The fog grew thicker, and Ellen let it overtake her. She knew she had made him understand, and she rested in the shelter of his arms.

Their secret was out. The whole town of Calypso seemed to have heard the news—"Ellen Brighton has Alzheimer's." It screamed like a newspaper headline.

Jake had a hard time accepting people's well-meaning sympathy. He felt as though they already considered her dead. If they couldn't avoid running into the Brightons altogether, acquaintances would stumble through uncomfortable, halting conversations, all but ignoring Ellen. She told Jake she felt like a leper.

And Jake was leprous by association. At the office the hush that descended on any room he entered was tangible. He could hear the sorrowful whispers that followed him down the street. The doctors had said to keep things as normal as possible. They hadn't mentioned that it would be impossible to do so once everyone knew her plight.

Sandra was a godsend. She offered Ellen sincere sympathy and then proceeded to cheer her up with her offbeat sense of humor. She somehow made it okay to joke about the crazy things Ellen did. She gave Ellen tacit permission to talk when she needed to—on the days she was able to articulate her thoughts—and to be silent without discomfort when words were too difficult.

Jake found himself looking forward to the evenings when Sandra visited. It was good to converse with someone who could give a simple answer without a struggle. She became a buffer between Jake and Ellen, diffusing the frustration they felt in trying to communicate with each other. And Sandra could always make him laugh. There was precious little laughter in his house these days.

5

Jake was dressed for work in suit and tie, but the sun had awakened him earlier than usual this morning, so he sat at the kitchen table enjoying a rare second cup of coffee and the morning newspaper. The sun was rising earlier each day and spring was making itself evident with a myriad of signs. The forsythia bush outside the kitchen window was burgeoning with fat ochre buds. If the temperature rose into the sixties as the forecast predicted, the bush would be a riot of yellow by the time Jake got home from work.

Jake was struck by the irony of it all. Such incongruity— the earth was bursting with new life, while Ellen was fading away. The days became longer as her memory grew shorter. New birth exploded in the world all around him, but in his home, life slowly decayed.

He had spent every day the past three months regretting they had ever told anyone that Ellen had Alzheimer's. It seemed that the day they admitted the truth, she began a helpless slide down the cliff of insanity. He knew it was irrational, but he felt sure that had they kept their secret, somehow it would not have become the grisly reality it now was.

In a strange reverse of nature, Ellen became more child-like as each day passed. She was temperamental and impatient. She wandered about the house with no direction and no goal. Jake brought her books from the library, and after reading only two or three pages, she lost interest.

She developed a strange habit of squirreling things away, hiding small objects throughout the house. She packed tea bags, still in their paper wrappers, into her jewelry box. She took pens and pencils from the desk by the phone and tucked them under the cushions on the sofa. If Jake caught her in the act of tucking away some mundane treasure, it angered her. So now when he came upon her secret caches, he put the contents away without comment. Two calculators were still missing from a desk drawer, and yesterday his favorite tie tacks and his wedding band had disappeared from the valet on his dresser. His wedding ring was loose, and he wore it only occasionally. They had never replaced the inexpensive rings they exchanged at their wedding, so the ring was valuable only in sentiment, but he hoped she hadn't hidden it too well.

With Jake's prodding, Ellen managed to keep the laundry done up and the house fairly tidy. She seemed to take pleasure in these familiar, methodical tasks. But Jake did most of the cooking. Ellen had ruined many meals before they decided the kitchen was best left to him. Also he was afraid for her to use the stove. It was a difficult adjustment for both of them. Ellen had always loved to cook, and Jake, though he was comfortable in the kitchen, had plenty of things he'd rather do.

Jake hired a woman to come in once a week and do the heavy cleaning, but he made every effort to involve Ellen in the everyday household tasks. She rode with him to the grocery store, and he asked her for suggestions when they planned menus and made shopping lists. In truth, it would have been infinitely easier to do it by himself, but he remembered the doctor's exhortation that he allow her to do as much as she possibly could for herself.

The doctor said Jake should be grateful she was still able to care for her physical needs, but it seemed to him that Ellen had regressed at an alarming rate. Her memory had declined daily—especially her recall of things they had done or said just moments before.

Brant called one night and talked to his mother for half an hour. Twenty minutes later Ellen turned to Jake and wondered aloud, "Why don't the kids ever call anymore?"

She had become apathetic and listless. She slept late and retired early, and the joy of life that had been so much a part of her personality was discernible only in rare, fleeting glimpses. Jake tried to keep their life busy and stimulating, but Ellen seemed content to sit at home night after night. She had had some embarrassing moments in public, and though she denied it, Jake felt certain that part of her reluctance to be with their friends or in any public setting was fear of further humiliation.

Ellen went through periods of deep depression when she could barely pull herself out of bed in the morning. Jake tried to get her to talk about her feelings, to get her pent-up anger and fears out in the open, but the frustration of trying to voice her feelings only made matters worse. He prayed with her, but though she never said so, Jake knew she was angry at God. And so at best, he could only hold her while she cried and cried.

One morning the telephone rang, and Ellen nearly jumped out of her skin. "What? What in the world?" she asked Jake with real fear in her eyes.

At first he didn't know what she meant. When it rang

again she pointed urgently into the air, vaguely in the direction of the phone. "That! That! Did you hear it?"

"The phone, you mean?"

"What is that?"

"The phone? Ellen! The telephone . . . you know, you talk to people on it." He was incredulous that she could not know something so basic. But when he realized that she truly didn't remember what a telephone was, he patiently took her to it and explained to her how it worked. By this time, the caller had given up and the bell was silent. But Jake was so upset he couldn't have spoken to anyone anyway.

Though she couldn't identify a common everyday object, Ellen seemed to sense how disturbed Jake was. She wrung her hands and paced the floor.

Jake insisted they go to worship services each Sunday morning as they had for all of their married years. Though Ellen was as apathetic about church as she was about everything else, she usually didn't argue when Jake reminded her that it was time to dress for church services. Their closest friends were there, and Jake drew strength and comfort from the encouragement they offered. It was one of the few places that Jake felt Ellen was accepted and treated as though she were still an adult . . . still human. After church their friends stopped by the pew in the back row where the Brightons sat and offered their greetings and concern. Ellen rarely responded with more than a nod or a wan smile, and Jake suspected it was because these people had become strangers to her. He rarely saw recognition in her eyes for anyone other than close family members.

Sandra was the exception. Ellen always knew her and was always happy to see her. And while she was no more vocal with Sandra than with Jake, she seemed to feel comfortable in Sandra's presence. Sandra tried to keep conversation a part of their relationship, but when Ellen clammed up, or when her speech made no sense, Sandra turned on the TV and they sat companionably together.

Jake was touched by the sacrifices Sandra made for both of them, and from her he learned much about relating to this new, silent Ellen.

Strangely, the jumbled words that had been such a glaring warning early in her illness manifested themselves less frequently now. Jake wondered if he had merely grown used to them, or if perhaps the mixed-up words abated simply because she was so silent now. Their fiery conversations and heated debates had virtually ended, and Jake missed them desperately. He made a conscious effort to describe his workdays to her in detail, to keep up his end of the conversation. This was difficult because she had become such a passive listener, and he feared that when she understood him, it was too painful for her to hear news of the schools and teachers she had once been so involved with. No matter how carefully he weighed his words, everything he said was a blatant reminder of all that she had lost. Her silence soon begot his.

⚬⚬⚬

Jana and Mark came to Calypso nearly every weekend after they found out about Ellen's illness. Jake was grateful for their company, and in the beginning Ellen seemed to enjoy having them there. But as she retreated further into silence, it became difficult for everyone. In one coherent moment, Ellen declared it was like a wake, only everyone was waiting for the corpse to die.

On the weekends Jake felt an obligation to entertain Mark and Jana, to cook for them and be the charming hostess that Ellen had once been. This did not come naturally to him, and he found himself becoming increasingly resentful—not of his daughter, but, unreasonably, of his wife for failing him like she had.

He saw the strain it put on Mark and Jana's marriage as well. They both worked long hours and their weekends were precious. Mark was a generous, caring man, but Jake could see that it was beginning to frustrate him to have to share his wife weekend after weekend. Jake heard them arguing one Saturday night when they thought he had already gone up to bed. Their overheard words cut him to the quick; yet he understood.

"Jana, I just want one day alone with you. Is that too much to ask?"

"This isn't fair and you know it, Mark. You're asking me to choose between you and Mom. I love you, but Mom needs me right now."

"I need you too, Jana! Your mom doesn't even know you're here half the time." Mark's voice rose in anger.

Jake could hear Jana crying. She spat the words out in choking sobs. "That was cruel, Mark! How can you be so cruel?"

He heard the back door slam and then Jana's muffled cries as she ran upstairs to the guest room.

The next morning Jake told them rather gruffly that there was no reason for them to come the following weekend. Jana argued halfheartedly, but Jake hushed her and closed the topic to discussion.

When Friday arrived and their car didn't pull into the driveway, Jake was surprised to find that he missed them. But soon his loneliness was filled with a good book, an hour spent puttering in the garage, and a leisurely walk with Ellen.

Jana called Jake after supper, and though the topic was left unmentioned, they let each other know through the warmth of their voices that everything was all right between them.

❧

Ellen had not driven since the day she "lost" her car at the mall. It wasn't something they had discussed, but there was an unspoken agreement that she would not drive again. It was difficult for both of them. Ellen knew she was burdening Jake, always having to be driven wherever she went. And yet neither was willing to risk the danger Ellen could be behind the wheel. She had always walked to school when the weather permitted, relishing the exercise, and she had continued to do so until she was forced to quit working. By then she had become withdrawn and antisocial, rarely going outside their home anyway, so Jake tried not to resent the times when he had to play chauffeur.

Late one afternoon when Jake was driving Ellen home from a dentist's appointment, she suddenly reached out and touched his arm. They were driving past Calypso's park, and Ellen pointed and pled with Jake.

"Oh, honey. Stop. Stop here. Let's stop here . . . at the . . . the . . ."

"The park?"

"Yes! The park. The park." She rolled the word around her tongue as though she were learning it for the first time.

Jake slowed the car and looked at Ellen. "Why? Why do you want to go to the park?"

"I don't know. It just . . . it just . . . it just sounds . . . fun. It's been a long time, hasn't it, honey? Or have we . . . have we. . . ?" She was unsure of even her memories now.

She looked so hopeful he couldn't say no. He turned into the last entrance and parked the car near the playground. Without a word Ellen got out of the car and walked toward the swings. Jake followed, hurrying to catch up with her. By the time he reached the sandy area where the swings were, Ellen had seated herself in the farthest swing and was pumping her legs, trying to get the swing in motion. Jake went around behind her and gave her a gentle shove.

"Hang on!" He pushed her again.

"Whee! Higher! Higher!" She squealed like a gleeful little girl.

How long had it been since they had laughed together like this? Jake's heart was full as he pushed her higher, faster. A gentle breeze rustled through the giant maples that shaded the park, and the waning sunlight cast bright, flickering shadows through the leaves. Finally he let the swing die down. Tenderly he brushed the windblown curls from her face, and leaning over he took her head in his hands and planted an upside-down kiss on her lips. She pulled his head down again and again to her own, kissing him hungrily. He wanted to stay here forever.

They lingered in the park—sitting side by side on the swings with fingers intertwined, swaying gently back and forth—until dark shadows fell across the grass, and the air grew cool. Then reluctantly they walked back to the car, refreshed by the gift of this sweet interlude.

Though their love for each other never faltered, nothing was really the same anymore. Every little incident, every task required a time of evaluation or a decision about what was safe, what was best for Ellen.

When the boys came home for Thanksgiving, they were angry at Jake for not telling them how fast their mother was failing. They had just been home in August and were shocked at how much she had deteriorated in the past three months.

After Ellen had gone to bed, Kyle stormed into the den where Jake was paying bills at his desk.

"Dad, why didn't you tell us it was this bad?"

"What do you mean, Kyle?" Jake was truly puzzled.

"Dad! She's a total zombie!" His face contorted and a sob escaped his throat.

Suddenly Jake realized that the changes that had come more gradually for him because he saw Ellen every day seemed monumental from Kyle's perspective. Also, Jake had tried to shield the boys from worry—when they called home, he made light of Ellen's problems and left out especially painful details.

"Oh, Kyle." Jake got up and came around his desk to embrace his son. He held Kyle while he poured his grief out in tears that stained Jake's shoulder and stabbed a knife in his heart. "Kyle, I'm sorry. I guess I didn't realize that you weren't seeing how bad it's gotten day by day. It's happened so gradually, and yet I know it didn't seem like Mom was all that confused the last time you were home."

"Dad, is she . . . is she always like this? Does she still have some good days?"

"Not really, Kyle. For a while she did, but it's been a long time . . . a long time."

Brant came into the den, took one look at Kyle's tear-stained face, and he broke down too.

"How can you stand this, Dad? Can't the doctors do something? This is like a nightmare. She's so . . . she's just not even my mom anymore."

"I know, Brant. I know. All we can do is love her. Mom can't help this—it's not her fault. We have to keep remembering that. We have to remember her the way she was."

Father and sons stood in a three-way embrace, drawing

strength and solace from one another. Then they went up to their separate rooms to wrestle with their own private agonies.

—∞—

The newest development in Ellen's decline was a small thing, but it bothered Jake immensely.

Ellen had always taken pride in her appearance. In many ways, Jake thought she was more beautiful in her forties than she had ever been. The beauty of her youth had mellowed into an elegance he found very attractive. Ellen had always put on makeup every morning; her hair was always neatly in place. She had loved to shop, and though she never spent a great deal of money on her clothes, she had wonderful taste and had always looked stylishly chic. Jake had been proud to have Ellen at his side.

Now, unless Jake reminded her, she forgot to even comb her hair in the morning. Fortunately, the last few years she had worn her short curls in a rather tousled style, so a comb was usually all it took to make her hair look presentable. But her makeup, if she remembered to apply it at all, was harsh and sloppy. She had taken to wearing sweatpants and mismatched shirts, pulling on whatever was handy, and, Jake suspected, whatever had the fewest buttons or zippers to wrestle with. If Jake laid out an outfit for the day, she was usually cooperative and dressed herself. But by the end of the day, her clothes were rumpled and stained from her carelessness. Jake felt guilty letting this relatively minor thing disturb him, but so much about Ellen had changed that this sloppiness now added embarrassment to his deepening pain.

Once again, Sandra came to the rescue. She took Ellen shopping and they bought several colorful, casual outfits that were easy to get in and out of. She also helped Ellen choose new, paler cosmetic colors that were more forgiving of Ellen's unsteady hand.

It was an improvement, but it still wasn't the Ellen that Jake was used to. But then nothing about her was the same anymore.

Though Ellen accepted Jake's affection, she rarely initiated it. He made an effort to embrace her, to greet her with a kiss each morning, and to hold her hand when they walked together in the evenings. The latter had become a necessity, to keep her from tripping on the uneven sidewalks. They walked almost every evening, just as they had for most of their marriage. It had been a time to catch up on the day's news and to connect with each other at the end of a busy day. It had also been a romantic time for them, walking hand in hand, sharing their love. Now it was becoming difficult for Jake to give and give and receive so little in return. He felt his love for her slipping away, and it terrified him.

Jake was becoming increasingly concerned about Ellen's safety around the house. He had no choice but to leave her alone while he went to work each day. He came home over the lunch hour and fixed her a sandwich or a salad. If Ellen was having a difficult day, or Jake was caught in a meeting, Sandra could sometimes get away from work to check on her. Mrs. Dobbs, the cleaning lady, had been persuaded to come for two half-days rather than one full day, so there was rarely a time when Ellen was alone for more than three or four hours. But much could happen in those few short hours, and Jake knew the time was coming when he would have to get someone to stay with Ellen every day while he was at work.

The time came sooner than he had anticipated. A staff meeting ran long one morning, and it was almost twelve-thirty when he finally got home for lunch. He parked in front of the house and ran inside, calling Ellen's name, worried that she would be hungry and fretting about his lateness. Usually she was sitting in front of the TV in the living room when he came home. And usually, in answer to his voice, she rose silently and came into the kitchen.

But today she did not appear. Jake searched the house, climbing the stairs to the second floor, then to the attic, calling for her with rising panic.

He ran out into the yard, screaming her name, not caring what the neighbors might think. He couldn't see her in the yard or the wooded area behind the house.

He ran back into the house through the garage, not sure where to turn next. Then he stopped short. In the dim light that filtered through the single window, he saw Ellen's profile behind the wheel of the car that had been hers.

He yanked open the car door, and with misplaced anger he pulled her roughly out of the seat.

"Ellen, what in the world are you doing?" he shouted.

She looked at him, perplexed. Then he saw the keys in her hand.

Jake grabbed the keys from her, then struggling for control and realizing it was himself he was angry with, he pulled her into his embrace. She began to cry. Over and over she wailed, "I thought I'd go . . . go . . . go . . . I thought I'd go . . . and go . . ."

He gently put his hand over her mouth to quiet her. "Ellen, you mustn't ever, ever get into the car when I'm not with you." He forced her to look at him. "Do you understand me? Never!" He scolded her like he had scolded Jana when she was small. And yet he knew that, unlike little Jana, Ellen would never learn another lesson. Her mistakes would never again be teachers.

Jake led Ellen into the house and fixed her a sandwich.

He spent the rest of his lunch hour fixing the door to the garage so it could be locked from the outside.

The next morning he made arrangements with the school to take a short leave of absence.

By week's end, Jake had a schedule of shortened hours at the office and had arranged for a woman from their church to come in to stay with Ellen during the mornings. It was far from ideal, and it wouldn't work indefinitely, but it was all Jake knew to do.

───◦∞◦───

A dismal turning point came just after Christmas. On a beautiful, crisp evening, feeling cooped up and in need of fresh air, Jake bundled Ellen up, and they walked several blocks around the neighborhood. It had been weeks since the weather was warm enough for them to take a walk. The sky was clear and full of stars, and it was good to get out in the brisk night air. Ellen was nostalgic, and in fragmented sentences she remembered aloud their first days living on Oaklawn. While she couldn't remember the current day of the week, she could recall events of their past—sometimes in surprising detail. This was ground on which Jake could meet her. He was feeling cheerful and optimistic with reminiscence.

They came back to the house, and standing by the closet in the front hall, Jake began to help Ellen out of her coat and gloves and scarf. Her face was flushed from the cold, and she looked like the Ellen of old. She gave him a winsome smile, and suddenly, he was overcome with desire for her. He dropped her coat to the floor and took her in his arms and kissed her hungrily. She didn't resist him, but looked at him questioningly. He took her hand and started up the steps to their bedroom.

Suddenly, Ellen sighed heavily, contentedly. Then in a clear but childish voice she said, "Oh, Daddy. So fun . . . fun. Can we go again? Walking? Maybe Mommy can come too . . . walk on the farm."

Jake stopped in his tracks. He turned, sick at heart, and looked down the steps at Ellen. Her eyes were gazing far away into the past. Her expression, her voice, were those of the child she had been forty years before. And in a moment of horrible realization, Jake knew that in Ellen's mind he had become her father. How could he take her into their marriage bed?

He turned slowly and guided her back down the steps. He fixed her a cup of warm milk, and while she sat in the kitchen sipping contentedly, Jake made up the twin beds in the bedroom on the ground floor. The room had most recently been Jana's. The wallpaper was a pale peach to match the ruffled comforters. The furniture was French provincial—a young girl's room. He brought down a few of Ellen's things from the bathroom and carried their alarm clocks down and plugged them in. Then he went to the kitchen and led Ellen to her new bed. He tucked her in and gave her a chaste kiss. She seemed unaware that anything was amiss. She burrowed under the blankets and closed her eyes.

Jake turned out the light and with heavy steps climbed to the attic. There he unplugged their lamps and gathered the contents of his night table. He took their toothbrushes and toiletries from the bathroom and moved these things down to Jana's room. He went back to the attic and gathered the clothes from Ellen's closet and drawers, burying his face in the soft fabrics, breathing in the faint scent of her perfume that lingered there. He arranged her things in the downstairs room and returned once more to the attic stairs and climbed them slowly.

He stood in the doorway and looked around the room,

now empty of their personal items. Through misted eyes, he saw the history of their love in this room. Sweet, intimate scenes floated like ghosts before him in the emptiness—a young couple sharing tender, romantic moments. Was that he . . . and Ellen? And now it had come to this? His throat was so full with emotion he felt a physical pain. Jake pulled the door shut, and with finality he put the timeworn key in the lock and turned it.

The next morning Jake awoke slowly. With half-closed eyes he looked groggily around the room, trying to remember why he was here on a narrow bed in Jana's old room. He turned over, squinting to block out the blinding sun that streamed in the east window. In a halo of sunlight, he saw Ellen's dark curls spread on the pillow in the bed next to his, and it all came back to him with terrible clarity. He had said goodbye to his lover last night. Never again would he know the intimate touch of her hands on his body. Never again would they share the oneness that had healed so many differences . . . the communion that had been such a joy to them for a quarter of a century.

Today he awoke to a new role. No longer friend and equal. No longer lover and confidant. Today he would begin to learn to be Ellen's protector . . . her keeper . . . her defender. Today she had become his child.

The weight of the task before him was oppressive. He felt small and unworthy. And worse, he wasn't sure he wanted the awesome responsibility—however precious his charge.

He threw back the covers and rose to face the morning. He would live one day at a time. It was an old cliché, but never had he understood its meaning so clearly.

Ellen began to stir beside him. Barely acknowledging him, she got out of bed and stumbled toward the kitchen. He followed her, pulling out a chair at the kitchen table for her, patting her shoulder as she sat down. He started coffee brewing and put two slices of bread into the toaster.

And so together—with much difficulty and many errors—they began to learn how to live with this horrible thing called Alzheimer's.

⚬⚬⚬

Spring came, summer passed, and when autumn again caused the leaves to drop from the trees, when everything shriveled and died, Jake finally felt that nature reflected Ellen's perverse metamorphosis. However, there was a beauty in nature's dying that Jake could not find in Ellen's.

Like the leaves falling one by one from their branches, Ellen died a little each day. A memory gone here, a sparkle of laughter there, until Jake hardly recognized the woman he loved.

6

Martin Sinclair was buried on a cold day in October. The wind swept through the trees in sporadic gusts, carrying the last dead leaves of autumn in frenzied circles, dipping and diving between the marble gravestones. The air was gray with a dense fog that muted the colors of the landscape to muddy greens and browns. The cemetery was wrapped in the stark tracery of a black iron fence. Against this backdrop the young husband and father was laid to rest.

The minister wore traditional black over his starched clerical collar. He stood before the people, intoning the ancient psalm: "The Lord is my shepherd; I shall not want. He maketh me to lie down in green pastures; he leadeth me beside the still waters; He restoreth my soul . . ."

The contingent of mourners swayed imperceptibly, a sea of dark coats on the side of the hill. The silence was broken now and then by muffled crying, the dark fabric relieved by the white flash of handkerchiefs.

". . . Yea, though I walk through the valley of the shadow of death, I will fear no evil: for thou art with me; thy rod and thy staff they comfort me."

But there was no comfort for the young widow sitting under the canopy with the casket, her young sons standing close to her on either side.

Julia Sinclair's eyes were red-rimmed, the skin around her nostrils ruddy and raw. She had shed a myriad of tears; there was no hiding that fact. But her eyes were dry now, her demeanor dignified. She sat erect, her dark blond hair pulled away from her face, her slender hands clasped in her lap. Her silence was incongruous with the voice that cried out in her mind, struggling to fathom the reality of this funeral.

It was still like a dream. The phone call . . . the panicked trip to the hospital. The words played an abrupt staccato in her mind: "Rain-slick roads . . . an accident . . . nothing we could do . . . Martin . . . gone . . . so sorry."

With agonizing pain, Julia saw again the stricken looks on the faces of Sam and Andy as they absorbed the news that their beloved dad was gone. At fourteen, Sam tried valiantly to be brave, and Julia marveled at how he had comforted her that first awful day. But he couldn't contain the sobs that wracked his adolescent body as he lay in his room that night. Julia stood at his door and longed for a magic word that would make the pain go away.

Andy, not yet twelve, was the tender one. He fell in her arms and cried inconsolably when she told him the news. It made Julia feel stronger, for the moment anyway, to be needed by someone hurting so badly.

She watched her sons now as the coffin was lowered into the dank hole. Sam's face was unreadable, but she feared she saw anger in Andy's eyes and in his posture. A crazy thought went fleetingly through her mind: *Martin will know how to handle this.*

". . . thou anointest my head with oil; my cup runneth

over. Surely goodness and mercy shall follow me all the days of my life: and I will dwell in the house of the Lord forever."

Oh, Martin. It's true. You're really gone. How will I ever make it without you? How will these boys live without their father?

The final prayer was offered, and the pallbearers walked out from under the canopy. The mourners began to swarm slowly toward the row of seats where Julia and the boys, her parents, and Martin's mother and brothers were seated. She nodded a mute reply to each expression of sympathy. She was moved by the sheer number of friends who had come to pay their respects to her husband. Martin was so loved. She felt small, each condolence given from a height above her. At one point she tried to stand, but the ground beneath her was soft under a grass carpet. Her heels sank into the uneven sod, and her legs would not hold her. She fell back onto the hard chair and buried her head in her hands.

Julia's parents had flown in from Indiana for the funeral, and they stayed at the apartment with Julia and the boys for a week. On the morning they were to fly back home, Julia woke suddenly before five. She tried to go back to sleep, but it was no use. Slumber eluded her. Pulling on a robe, she padded into the kitchen and started a pot of coffee brewing. As much as she had needed her mother and father at her side during these difficult days, she knew the real work of grieving for Martin could not begin until they had gone. For that reason, she was anxious to say goodbye and begin the task.

She took a cup of coffee to the table by the big kitchen window and sat down. The apartment that had been her home—their home—for over a decade was a renovation in

Chicago's old Lakeview neighborhood, one that the real estate listings had touted as having "lots of character." And in spite of the temperamental plumbing and the inefficient utilities, Julia had grown to love the rooms' high ceilings and creaking hardwood floors. She looked through the kitchen into the open living and dining areas beyond, and memories came flooding back. It seemed as though Martin had been gone forever—and yet it also seemed as though he might walk into the room at any moment, his booming voice holding a smile that one could hear.

"Up so early?" Her father's voice brought her back to the moment. He was freshly showered and smelled of the shaving soap he had used for as long as she could remember.

"Oh, I couldn't sleep. I'm sorry if I woke you."

"It's okay. I couldn't sleep either. Are you okay?"

"I'm dreading this day . . . I'll miss you and Mom. And yet . . . I know that until I face this apartment alone and see how the boys are really handling all this, I can't begin to . . . to recover." She broke down then. "Oh, Dad . . . how can I ever recover? I just never thought this could happen to me. I never thought I'd be alone." Panic rose in her as she faced the reality of the life before her. "I can't raise these boys by myself! I can't do it, Dad! They need a father! They need Martin!"

Her father came around and stood behind her, his hands firmly on her shoulders. His voice was thick with emotion, but he spoke with the strength that Julia remembered from her childhood. His words poured over her like a soothing ointment.

"Julie . . . oh, Julie." He hadn't called her that for twenty years. "Honey, I don't know why God has seen fit to put you through this. If I could take away the hurt . . . if I could bring Martin back, you know I'd do it in a minute. But I can't." He struggled to control his own emotions, and when he spoke again, the strength came from somewhere outside of himself. "I know this, though, you're not in this alone, honey. You know that God is able, above and beyond all that you can imagine, to take you through this. I have not a doubt that Mom and I are leaving you in good hands when we get on that airplane today. Don't you forget that."

"I know, Dad. I know. Just . . . please pray for me."

"Oh, honey. We'll be praying for you every single day."

She stood to meet his embrace. "Thank you, Dad. Thank you for everything." For more than forty years her daddy had always been there when she needed him, and never had she needed him more than today.

Six months later she stood in the same kitchen surveying the apartment through new eyes. Her father's words had proven true. Though there had been times of despair, the Lord had comforted her in miraculous ways. But the memories of Martin were painfully close here in these rooms they had shared.

At first it had comforted her to be reminded of him at every turn. She had tried to keep their family traditions alive—taking the boys to breakfast at the Pancake House before church each Sunday, grocery shopping together every Wednesday night, out for pizza afterward. She had renewed their season tickets to the symphony and invited a friend to use Martin's ticket. She had continued to jog the route they had jogged together each morning.

But now she had begun to be angry that he wasn't there sharing these places with her. She had begun to resent whatever friend sat in Martin's seat at the symphony. She dreaded the jogs because they only reminded her of how lonely she was.

The apartment was full of Martin. He had had such a presence about him. Without being obnoxious or overbearing, Martin had held court in any room he entered. He was charming and affable, and he had been the indisputable head of the Sinclair family.

Three months after the funeral, Julia had cleaned out Martin's closet and packed up his toiletries from the bathroom. In a fit of anger, she'd rearranged the furniture in their bedroom, grunting and huffing to move the huge bed by herself. She took his sailing trophies off the mantel and threw them in a box. How dare he leave her alone like this! How dare he leave his things to remind her, everywhere she turned, of the great love they had shared. She tried to banish his ghosts from the apartment. But still his presence permeated every room.

The boys were haunted by memories too. Sam and Andy both refused to sit in Martin's big recliner in the living room. It had been "Martin's chair." When he was alive, the boys had argued over the chair if Martin wasn't home and wouldn't have dared to sit there if he was. Now that they were free to take it over, it was as though the chair was abhorrent to them. Not understanding their feelings, Julia made a terrible mistake about that recliner one night.

They were watching a movie in the living room when Sam and Andy started to argue over the couch they were both sitting on. Sam sprawled across the length of it, his huge feet on Andy's lap. When Andy complained, a shoving match ensued, and Sam pushed him to the floor. This made Julia furious.

"Sam, if you want to stretch out so bad, sit in the recliner. It's sitting there empty—the best seat in the house. You can stretch all you want."

"No, Mom. I was here first."

"Fine. Then sit up so Andy will have a place to sit."

"Why don't you make him move?"

"Because he's not the one who wants to take up the entire couch."

Sam ignored her and stayed recumbent on the couch.

"Sam, get off right now."

No response. The movie blared in the background, and Sam feigned interest in the action on-screen.

"Hey!" She got his attention. "Don't make me tell you again. Go sit in the recliner."

"Forget it. I'll sit up." He made a halfhearted effort to start moving.

She was angry. "No. It's too late now. You just lost your couch privileges, buddy. You sit in the recliner."

He stood and started to move a straight chair from the table in the adjoining dining room, dragging it off the rug and across the bare wood.

"Sam! You're scratching up the floor. Don't drag that in here. What's wrong with the recliner? Just sit there."

"No!" He was so adamant she should have sensed it was something more than just losing his place on the couch. But she only heard his defiance. He was standing right in front of the recliner now, and she gave him a shove that neatly seated him in the big chair.

The anguished cry that rose from his throat was barely human. It was the wail of an injured animal. It was the wail of a boy who had sat in the lap of a ghost. He struggled to pull his gangly body from the chair and fled to his room, sobbing.

Julia was shocked. She turned off the TV and stared at Andy as though he might have an explanation. He began to cry then, too. Through his tears he tried to make her understand.

"Mom, you shouldn't have made Sam sit in Dad's chair.

That's Dad's chair. Dad should be sitting there. It's not fair."

Julia pulled his head to her shoulder and sat with him until his sobs subsided.

She ruffled his hair affectionately. "You'd better get to bed, bud. We'll finish the movie tomorrow, okay? You gonna be all right?"

He nodded.

She steeled herself and went down the hall and knocked softly on Sam's door.

His reply was a muffled "Yeah?"

He was lying on his stomach in bed, the pillow bunched into a ball under his chin. She rubbed his back tentatively, testing his response. He didn't reject her.

"Sam, I'm sorry . . . it wasn't about the chair, was it?"

"Huh-uh."

"It's about Dad? That's what Andy says."

"Andy's pretty smart." He gave her a sad half-grin, then turned serious. "Mom, I'm kinda mad at God. I don't understand why He let Dad die. You and Dad always told us that God loves us, and He wants what's best for us. But I don't see how it could be best for us to lose Dad."

"Oh, Sam." Julia sighed and sent up a quick prayer—an SOS to heaven for the right answer to give this searching young man. "Honey, I was mad at God for a while too. And I won't pretend to understand why this happened to us. I'm like you . . . I can't believe God thought it was best for Dad to die and leave us to go on without him. But I think it's what we do now that it has happened that is important. Maybe the laws of nature are more to blame for Dad's death than God is. I truly believe God is great enough that He could have reached down and saved Dad from the wreck if He had chosen to. But for some reason we'll probably never understand, He didn't. And we have to go on from there.

The Bible says that all things work together for good to those who love God, and I'm just trusting that that's true." She rubbed her son's back as she spoke and prayed that God would meet Sam with the answers she couldn't provide. Strangely, she had tried to comfort herself with those same words, but they had not taken root in her heart and mind.

They talked for an hour then—mother and son. Sam spilled out hurts and fears that had been locked inside for all the months since he had lost his dad.

Late that night, alone in bed, Julia made the decision to leave Chicago. They would go somewhere—away from this city of memories—and begin to build new memories of their own.

7

Christmas had become a time of great sadness at the Brighton house. Jake dreaded it for weeks beforehand and could not bring himself to decorate the house in any way. It seemed a sacrilege to adorn the house for celebration when there was more cause for mourning.

When Brant and Kyle came home two days before Christmas, they went to the garage for the ladder and boxes of lights, and without consulting Jake, they spent the afternoon stringing lights on the house and hanging their stockings on the mantel. They put the tree in its stand in the front hall but decided to wait until Jana came to hang the ornaments.

Jake tried to allow their loving efforts to lift his own spirits, but he felt powerless to escape the depression that engulfed him. The struggle to reconcile his present circumstances with God's goodness had exhausted him. He knew, in a place deep within himself, that God was in this somewhere. Or at least He was with him in this. When he and Ellen had buried Catherine, they had known the assurance

117

of blessing even in the sorrow. That blessing had come in the formation of a greater bond of love between husband and wife, and in the fulfilled hope of more children. But Ellen's disease offered neither the bond nor the hope. He toiled to find even a hint of God's hand in all this, but he came up empty. Yet somewhere, somehow, that deep river of faith continued to flow in him and kept him from utter despair.

———

Jana and Mark arrived on Christmas Eve afternoon. A few hours later, they were putting the final touches on the Christmas tree when Howard and MaryEllen pulled into the driveway. With MaryEllen's arrival, the kitchen became a haven of homey sounds and spicy aromas.

Jana had grown close to her grandmother since Ellen's illness, and they relished this time together. Jana still needed her mother, and sensing this, MaryEllen had become the confidante that Ellen could no longer be. They baked cookies and breads, talking as fast as they stirred. Ellen sat at the kitchen table and watched, but she showed no interest in joining them. Still, it was a comfort to her mother and her daughter to have her near. She spoke quietly now and then, as if to herself. And though Jana and MaryEllen could make no sense of her words, they responded whenever she spoke and tenderly included her in their conversation. Around nine, Jake came and put Ellen to bed. Grandmother and granddaughter talked late into the night. When the last loaves of bread were cooling on the kitchen counter, they got the turkey ready to be put in the oven early the next morning. Then exhausted, they went upstairs to bed.

On Christmas Day they laid a feast on the oak table in the dining room. The table was set with Ellen and Jake's wedding china and an elegant centerpiece of holly and tall white candles. There was much love around that table, and Jake felt his spirits begin to lift. Ellen, though, seemed oblivious to the faces gathered around her. In their own way, each of them ministered love and acceptance to her. They were trying so hard to break through—to reach her in whatever faraway place she dwelled. Jake willed her to acknowledge them, to show some glimmer of recognition. It would mean so much if she would just give Jana a smile, or give the boys that teasing grin she had always reserved for them.

But Ellen existed on another plane. After dinner she sat on the sofa staring at the TV, or she paced between the kitchen and the conservatory. She had developed a shuffling gait that made her look older than her fifty years. Yet in repose, her face was still beautiful—as smooth and free of creases as someone ten to fifteen years younger. In some ways, her looking so young and beautiful made her affliction seem all the more cruel.

As he did every morning, Jake had lovingly applied lipstick and blush to Ellen's passive face. She was wearing the soft violet dress he had laid out for her that morning. He had brushed her hair till it shone, and except for the vacant stare that marred her eyes, she truly looked pretty. If it meant nothing to her, it comforted him to have her look attractive and well kempt.

In the afternoon when it was time to open gifts, Jake coaxed Ellen to sit in the overstuffed chair near the fireplace. The family gathered around her as though she were the centerpiece of this celebration, and in a subdued spirit, they opened their gifts.

Ellen began to open the brightly wrapped packages that Jake put in her lap. She slowly, painstakingly took off each ribbon, and taking care not to tear the paper, she took it off, folded it neatly, and stacked it by her chair. She held each item up and inspected it quizzically, as though wondering what to do with it. She opened a bright blue sweatsuit from Jake and began to pull it on over the clothes she already wore. Jake gently took the outfit from her, and with a quiet explanation, he folded it and laid it beside her chair. Ellen opened nightgowns, a sweater, and from Jana, a little porcelain bird for her collection. This made her smile, pleasing Jana immensely. As she opened each package, Jake patiently explained who it was from until Ellen nodded a response.

Ellen laid down the last gift in the small pile that had collected at her side. Then she looked around the room, and with a tiny smile of recognition, she said softly in her jumbled way, "Thanks you . . . thanks you to . . . to. . . . Good. Good."

Then to Jake's astonishment Ellen bowed her head and began to pray. With clarity and eloquence, the jumbled syllables were suddenly replaced with clearly enunciated words of praise. "Oh, Father, thank you," she prayed. "Thank you for this day you have made. Thank you for this love you have given us. Thank you, Lord . . . thank you . . ." Her voice trailed off, but a serene smile remained on her face.

Jake was stunned. He looked around the room, wondering if anyone else had heard her. The tears that streamed down Jana's cheeks, the emotion on Howard's and MaryEllen's faces, told him that he wasn't imagining it.

Not wanting to spoil the reverence of the moment, but needing to understand what had just happened—wondering even if a miracle had taken place, a healing of some sort—Jake touched Ellen's hand.

She looked up at him, but the vacant confusion was still in her eyes, and the smile she gave him was not a smile of recognition. Jake's momentary disappointment was quickly replaced with a sense of awe. He had witnessed a miracle. While Ellen's mind was wasting away, he—they all—had been offered a glimpse of the spirit within her that communed with an eternal God. It was an answer to Jake's prayer. She had acknowledged their presence. She had felt their love. And she still knew her God. It was enough for Jake.

───※───

In March, the district conference for school administrators was to convene in Springfield. Jake planned to leave early on a Monday morning and would not return until Wednesday evening. It struck him that in all the years since Ellen had gotten sick, he had never once left her for more than a few hours. Now, two retired nurses from their church came in each day, sharing shifts, and Sandra stayed with Ellen on the evenings Jake had meetings. He had been able to go back to a full workday, but his social life—and Ellen's—had virtually come to an end.

Now he was faced with a dilemma. The school district had been incredibly supportive. They had given Jake many hours away from the office when Ellen's needs were his first priority. But Jake felt he could not continue to give his job such halfhearted attention and still feel worthy of keeping it. And this conference was not optional.

He had considered driving Ellen to the Randolphs', but MaryEllen had fallen in the garden the week before and broken her wrist. Jake didn't feel right about placing the burden of Ellen's care on them. After all, they were both almost eighty.

Sandra had offered to take a few vacation days from her job to stay with Ellen, but Jake didn't feel right about that either. She had already sacrificed so much for Ellen—for him, really.

He didn't even call the kids because he knew they would,

without hesitation, make arrangements to get off work or out of school and come as soon as they could. He didn't want the burden on them either.

On the Wednesday before he was to leave, he finally called a number that he found in the Yellow Pages for a home nursing service. The price was higher than they could really afford, but the agency would send a registered nurse out on Monday morning who could stay with Ellen the entire time. She would cook for Ellen and do her laundry as well. Jake decided the peace of mind was worth it. Besides, he really didn't have a choice.

Monday the doorbell rang precisely at eight A.M., and Jake opened the door to a cheerful, grandmotherly woman. He had expected the traditional white uniform and nursing cap, but she was dressed in casual street clothes.

"Hello," Jake said, extending his hand. "I'm Jake Brighton. Please come in."

"Thank you. Anne Grady with Homecare."

"Yes. I'm very grateful you could come. Come on in, and I'll introduce you to my wife. They did tell you that Ellen has Alzheimer's?"

"Oh yes. I have all the information right here." She patted the bag that hung heavily from a strap on her shoulder. "I've worked with quite a few Alzheimer's patients before, Mr. Brighton. I'm sure everything will go just fine. How long has your wife—may I call her Ellen?"

"Yes, please. She'll be more comfortable with that."

"How long has Ellen been ill?"

"She was diagnosed about three years ago. But we were beginning to see symptoms probably a year or more before that."

"Is she still coherent? Does she recognize people?"

"Not very often. Once in a while she seems to know the kids when they come home. I think sometimes she knows who I am . . . or at least I'm a familiar face to her. But she rarely calls any of us by name or even speaks directly to anyone anymore. She's fairly quiet actually. When she does speak, we usually can't make any sense of what she's saying. The doctors say she is in the early stages of dementia. They tell me I'm fortunate that she's so quiet and subdued. 'Fortunate' seems a strange word for it." He didn't mean to be maudlin. He apologized and continued with the instructions.

"Ellen still takes care of most of her personal needs. She dresses herself if I lay out her clothes and keep reminding her to get dressed. She can bathe herself if I run the bath water. I do stay with her, though, because she fell asleep in the tub once . . . I don't trust her alone. Let's see . . . what else do you need to know? Her medications are on top of the kitchen cupboard, and I've written down the schedule and dosages. She feeds herself, but she won't eat unless you put the food right in front of her, and sometimes even then you have to keep reminding her to eat. She seems to be getting thin, so I try to give her frequent snacks. There are sandwich fixings in the refrigerator and plenty of soups in the cupboards. Ellen likes salads for lunch and there are vegetables in the crisper for that. Please make yourself at home. I hope I've stocked the cupboards with some things you like."

"Oh, I'll be fine. Don't worry about me. Would you have any objections if I took Ellen out in my car?"

"Not at all; she would probably enjoy that."

"Does she need help walking?"

"Oh, we usually walk each evening—just around the neighborhood—and she likes to hold my arm. She doesn't break any records for speed, but she does pretty well. Around the house she gets along fine on her own."

"She goes to the bathroom by herself?"

"Yes, yes. Really, except for cooking and bathing she does amazingly well. I do help her with her hair and put a little lipstick on her. She was always so careful about how she looked."

They had come to the living room where Ellen sat staring at the television. Jake went over to her and touched her shoulder. She looked up at him blankly.

"Ellen, this is Anne Grady. She's going to stay with you while I'm in Springfield. Remember, I told you I have some meetings there?"

In spite of his conscious efforts not to, Jake had begun speaking to Ellen in the tone one would use with a small child.

Anne Grady sat down beside Ellen and took her hand. "Hello, Ellen. How are you?"

Ellen looked at her but did not respond.

"I'm Anne. I'll be here if you need anything, okay?"

Ellen turned and looked at Jake. "Oh, oh, oh, oh, okay." So often now, Ellen sounded like a broken record. She spoke a syllable and then couldn't seem to turn it off. It irritated Jake more than anything she did. Ellen turned back to the TV, and Anne Grady patted Ellen's leg affectionately and rose to her feet.

"I think we'll do just fine, Mr. Brighton. Now if you would show me around the house, I'll get settled so you can be on your way."

⚬⚬⚬

It felt strange to be on the road. Except for short trips to visit the kids or to the farm to see Howard and Mary-Ellen, Jake and Ellen had stayed close to home for the better part of three years. When they first found out Ellen was sick, Jake had offered to take her to all the exotic places they had dreamed about—Europe, the Caribbean—but Ellen told him she just wanted to be home. So they had made the most of every minute in the house they both loved. Now, he felt oddly vulnerable without Ellen by his side.

He kept thinking of additional things he should have told Mrs. Grady, despite the three pages of detailed notes and phone numbers he had left with her. At the last minute, he had called Jana and told her about the arrangements so she wouldn't worry if she tried to call home. Still, he was afraid he had forgotten something important.

As soon as he checked into the hotel where the conference was being held, he called home to see how things were going. Since everything seemed to be under control, Jake relaxed a little and found he enjoyed the morning's meetings.

On Tuesday the weather was beautiful, so when Jake got out of his last meeting at five, he went for a run on the hotel's jogging path that followed the curving course of a man-made lake. Surprisingly, the path was deserted this late in the afternoon. As Jake breathed in the air that blew across the water, he breathed in a freedom that he had forgotten existed. It was liberating to have a few days laid out before him—hour upon hour—with obligations to no one but himself and the job he loved. He felt physically lighter with each step he took, as though a great load were being lifted from his back. It came as a revelation—just how desperately he needed this hiatus from the grave burden of Ellen's care.

He came back to his room, showered, and went to the hotel restaurant for a late dinner. He read the newspaper over chicken cordon bleu, lingering at the table, relishing each precious second of time that was his alone. After an hour, he paid the tab and started back to his room. Before getting on the elevator, he stopped by the desk in the lobby to inquire about the next day's schedule. When Jake happened to mention his name, the concierge turned to the large board behind him.

"Oh, Mr. Brighton. I believe we have a message for you." He handed Jake a folded slip of paper bearing his room number.

Jake opened the paper and read the ominous words: "Call home immediately."

The elevator seemed to take forever. Jake stepped inside and blindly pushed the button for his floor. What could have happened? Had Mrs. Grady found the task too difficult and backed out on him? Was something wrong with Ellen? Knowing Jake's circumstances, no one would leave him a message like that unless it was truly an emergency.

"Oh, dear God. Let it be a mistake. Please. Let it be a terrible mistake."

The elevator crawled to the fourth floor and opened onto the long corridor. Jake hurried down the hall, fumbling for his keys. He unlocked the door and went to the phone on the bedside table. The message light was blinking red. He grappled with the buttons on the phone, trying to get an outside line. Finally he heard the tone, and with a sense of foreboding, he dialed home.

Jana answered the phone.

"Jana?" Why was she there? "It's Dad. What's wrong?"

"Oh, Dad! Thank goodness you called! Mom's . . . gone." He could tell by her voice that she was near tears.

"What? What are you saying, Jana?"

Her words tumbled out in a rush. "The nurse was fixing Mom a snack in the kitchen this afternoon, and when she came back to the living room Mom wasn't there. She looked everywhere in the house and outdoors too, but Mom was just gone. We've been trying to reach you since about five. Oh, Dad, I'm so worried. Everybody in the neighborhood is looking for her, but we don't have a clue as to where she might be. Nobody has seen her."

"Do you mean she just walked out of the house by herself? She's never done that, Jana! Are you sure she's not right around the house there or out in the yard? I can't imagine her going off on her own like that. She's never done that before."

"The front door was open when Mrs. Grady came to give her her snack. I don't know what else could have happened."

"Have you called the police?"

"Yes. They said they would put out an alert, but we haven't heard anything from them yet. Oh, Dad, what are we going to do?"

"I don't know, Jana. Do the boys know?"

"I just got ahold of Brant, and he's going to try to find Kyle and come home right away. Mark is out searching with the neighbors. She couldn't have gotten very far, could she, Dad? She can't even walk that well."

"I don't know, honey. Just try to stay calm, okay? I'm packing right now, and I'll be home as soon as I can. It took me about three hours to get up here so it might be late when I get there. Oh, I knew I shouldn't have left her. I can't believe this is happening. Where is Mrs. Grady now?"

"We sent her home. She was really upset, Dad; she feels terrible. Do you think maybe she wasn't watching her very well?"

"I don't know, Jana. I can't imagine how this could have happened!" A cloud of guilt descended and nearly overwhelmed him. How could he have left her? What was he thinking? With difficulty, he composed himself. "Okay, I'm going to hang up and get on the road. You're doing great, honey. Just stay by the phone . . . and pray. She'll have to show up soon."

"I know, Dad, but it's getting dark."

Macabre thoughts filled Jake's mind as he flew through the night toward home. He saw Ellen's twisted body lying in a ditch, or worse, floating on a black river. With each vision, he pressed his foot harder to the accelerator.

"How could I have let this happen? Oh, I knew I shouldn't have left her. Oh, Ellen . . . poor Ellen. Please, God. Wherever she is . . . be with her . . . help her. *Please*."

Jake drove for miles berating himself. He remembered the day he had found her in the car in the garage, and he chastised himself for not taking the incident more seriously. Surely that had been a clue that she was prone to wander. How could he have been so stupid? Would his children ever forgive him if anything happened to their mother? Could he ever forgive himself? He alone was to blame. This was all his fault. He had no business running off so far away, lounging in a hotel when Ellen was so ill. What kind of husband was he anyway?

Though he was breaking the speed limit, the landscape seemed to crawl by. He wanted to stop and call home to see if they had found her yet, but he dared not waste a precious moment. And so he drove on.

"Oh, dear God. Is this how it's all going to end? No! Please, not yet! I'm not ready to lose her . . . not like this."

8

It was ten thirty-five when Jake turned onto Oaklawn. Even before he was in sight of their house, he saw the line of cars parked on the street in front. He recognized Brant's car and Mark and Jana's. Even Howard and MaryEllen had driven in. Sandra's car was there and several other vehicles he didn't recognize.

All the lights inside and out were burning, giving the old house a festive look, as though a happy party were raging inside.

Jake parked on the driveway and ran up the front walk. Jana met him at the door.

"Oh, Dad. Thank God you're home."

"Did you find her?"

"No! Not a clue. The boys and Mark are still out looking, as are some of the neighbors—the Grants and Bob Markham." She lowered her voice to a whisper and motioned toward the living room. "We finally made Grandpa come inside—we were worried about him. He walked the neighborhood for two hours. Dad, I don't know what else to do." She broke down then and sobbed in Jake's arms.

"Jana, you've all done exactly what you should. I couldn't ask for more. I'm going to make a couple of phone calls, and I want you to go up and try to get some sleep. We're going to have a long day ahead of us. Now, has anyone called the hospital to see if she's shown up there?"

"Yes. But that was a couple of hours ago. Do you think we should try again?"

"Yes. I'll do that. And I'm going to call the police department myself. You get some sleep now, honey."

"I'll try. But first I'll go make up the bed for Grandma and Grandpa."

Jake went into the living room and spoke with Howard and MaryEllen, Sandra, and the others who had gathered to help. Without prompting, they gathered and circled the room, joining hands.

"God," Jake prayed aloud, "you know where Ellen is right now. Oh, Lord, we put her in your hands. Please watch over her, and keep her warm, Lord. It's so cold out there tonight . . ." Jake's voice faltered, and he felt Jana and Sandra squeeze his hands on either side. Their touch strengthened him to go on. "And give us wisdom to know where to look for her. Please, God, . . . we need you. We need you now." They stood that way for a long time, heads bowed, bound together. Finally Jake cleared his throat and broke from the circle. There were no words to express his thanks, but he tried. Then he sent everyone home. He told Ellen's parents that Jana had their bed ready, and they wearily climbed the stairs.

Sandra stayed, tidying up the kitchen and offering moral support while Jake went to the telephone and dialed the hospital. They had nothing to report. He was still making phone calls when the boys came in just before two in the morning. Sandra gathered her things and left with a promise to return at daylight. The searchers had gone home for some rest and something to eat, and they had arranged to start again at daybreak.

The police came to the house and talked to Jake and asked him for a photograph of Ellen to fax to the surrounding towns.

Jake had called everyone he could think of who might have seen Ellen, but it seemed no one knew anything.

At three A.M. a light rain began to fall. Jake sat half propped up on the couch in the living room, hope deflating in him like a pierced balloon. He watched a silent television screen display the time and temperature. It was fifty-two degrees. Jake willed the thermometer not to drop any lower. And he prayed as he had never prayed in all his life.

He finally dozed off around four, and when the first gray light of morning filtered through the curtains, he woke with a start. He got up and took a quick shower to steel himself for the day ahead.

He tiptoed into the kitchen and put on a pot of coffee. Within minutes the boys joined him, and by the time they finished toast and coffee, the whole household was stirring and cars were pulling into the drive.

Jake called the hospital again. Still no luck. Then he called the police. They had no new information but assured Jake they were doing everything possible to locate Ellen.

Jake's plan was to leave Jana and MaryEllen to manage the phone and send the rest of the searchers in different directions through the neighborhood. He felt they could cover the most territory that way. He asked Howard to search the large yard and surrounding woods once again.

Jake stepped out the back door. The morning chill filled him with new terror. It was barely fifty degrees. Ellen had been wearing sweatpants and a light sweatshirt. Could she possibly have survived a night in this weather?

Jake began walking the route that he and Ellen usually took on their strolls through the neighborhood each evening. He had never felt so solitary walking that path. He tried not to think that he may never walk this way with Ellen again. He longed for the warmth of her hand in his, the familiar weight of her body against his as he wended his way alone down this street that they loved.

It was odd how the trees, gardens, and yards in which he and Ellen had always found such beauty now took on an ominous, foreboding aura. His imagination played tricks on him; bent tree limbs began to look like human limbs. Jake walked to the point where he and Ellen usually turned back and began to retrace his steps, straining to see what he might have missed on the first pass.

When he walked through the front door forty-five minutes later, the house was in bedlam. Jana was on the phone, tears of joy and exhaustion mixing on her cheeks. Mary-Ellen was trying to hush the cheers and excited questions of the others so that Jana could hear to write down a phone number. She waved her hands futilely, her arm still encased in a cast.

When Jana saw Jake, she shouted, her voice breaking, "They found her, Dad! They found her!"

"Where? Is she okay?"

With her hand over the receiver, Jana explained as quickly as she could. "She was at the school. This is Mrs. Linmeyer. When she got to school this morning, she found Mom sitting on the front steps waiting for the doors to open." Jana broke down and handed the phone to her dad. "Here, you talk to her."

"Carolyn?"

As he listened to Carolyn's story, relief flowed visibly through him. Ellen had wandered the twelve blocks to the school—a route she had walked many days when she was teaching—and apparently had spent the night on the steps. She was cold and wet, hungry and confused, but she was unharmed.

Jake and Jana drove to the hospital where Carolyn had taken Ellen. She was on an examination table in the emergency ward. Someone had called Dr. Morton, and he met Jake in the hallway.

"Hi, Jake." There was sympathy in his voice. "Pretty tough night, huh?"

Jake nodded wearily. "Pretty tough. Is she okay?"

"She's going to be fine. I'm having them start an IV right now—just as a precaution. She's really in pretty good shape considering what she's been through. She keeps saying she has to get to class—she was such a dedicated teacher."

It was Jerry's way of giving dignity to the humiliation of the situation. Jake blessed him for remembering Ellen as she had been before.

He went then to Ellen. He heard her voice before he saw her. He was amazed at the clarity of her words, however irrelevant they were. Over and over she was pleading, in a voice that was almost singsong, "Somebody, please, I've got to get to school. I've got to get to class. Please, somebody." When she saw Jake she reached for his hand.

Jake spent the days that followed in turmoil. He had arranged to take yet another week's vacation from work. There were decisions with far-reaching consequences that had to be made in seven short days.

Ellen could no longer stay alone for even a minute. He would never forgive himself if this happened again. Or, God forbid, something worse. He made lists of options and alternatives, determining advantages and disadvantages of each choice; he spent hours on the telephone; he searched his heart, trying to discern his motives. And after three days, he was no closer to an answer than he had been before.

In desperation, he dug through his desk drawer and found the sheet from Dr. Gallia's prescription pad—given him those few years back, which now seemed like an eternity ago. "The Alzheimer's Association" was scribbled on the note with a toll-free number to call. What could it hurt? Jake picked up the phone and dialed the number. When he finally worked his way through the maze of recordings and heard a human voice, Jake felt he had been thrown a lifeline.

Here were answers to his questions. Here were people who understood exactly what he was going through. Here were people who amazingly seemed to know Ellen. Through the referrals they gave him, Jake discovered there was a nursing care center right in Calypso that specialized in the care of Alzheimer's patients. Jake had driven past the sprawling complex of buildings a hundred times. The modern sign in front declared "Parkside Manor—The Place That Cares." But never had Jake thought this place had any relevance to him. If he gave it any thought at all, he had pictured rows of rocking chairs, a wrinkled, gray head nodding in each one.

Reluctantly, Jake made an appointment to speak with the administrator the following Tuesday. He learned that while there was a waiting list for private rooms, a semiprivate room was available within the month. But he would have to decide quickly.

Parkside had a special unit for Alzheimer's patients, and Jake was impressed with the services that were available. The rooms were beautiful, the hallways clean and uncluttered. The nurses and aides were friendly and attentive. Only one thing tainted the professional environment—the residents. If he had walked through these halls four years earlier, before need colored his view, he would have been sickened . . . appalled by this distorted segment of humanity that he had never before given a thought to. He saw a dozen

Ellens—staring blankly at the television, walking down the hallways with that characteristic shuffle, mumbling to themselves as they paced the solarium. Through an open door he heard a belligerent voice screaming obscenities, and the calm, patient reply of an attendant. He saw men and women in their seventies and eighties, and a few, like Ellen, who looked barely fifty.

Could he bring Ellen to this place and walk away? Could he live with himself if he abandoned her here? Oh, of course, he would visit her every day. He would continue to care for her in every way he could, but would she see it as abandonment? Would she sink further into dementia in a place like this? Or was there help for her here? These questions roiled in Jake's head, and he left the place deeply troubled.

∞

The sound of breaking glass shattered the two A.M. silence. Jake sat upright and saw immediately that Ellen was not in her bed beside his. The door that he was careful to close tightly each night was ajar, and he heard Ellen's low moans coming from the kitchen. He stumbled through the dimly lit hallway and into the kitchen.

Ellen sat on the floor, blood from an ugly gash on the palm of her hand staining her nightgown. The jagged shards of a broken juice glass surrounded her, and she held her hand gingerly while she rocked back and forth, wailing like a frightened child.

Jake grabbed the broom and quickly swept a path for his own bare feet. Then he picked Ellen up and carried her to the safety of the living room. The wound in her hand was fairly deep and would need stitches. He wrapped a clean dishcloth around it to stanch the flow of blood and dressed her for the trip to the emergency room—her second one in just over a week.

In the waiting room, Ellen fell asleep on Jake's shoulder. There had been a car accident and the emergency room was full. They waited for nearly an hour before Ellen was ushered, groggy and confused, into a treatment room. Jake sat beside her and held her other hand while the doctor put eight stitches in the wound. The doctor gave her a sedative, and Ellen slept through most of the ordeal.

When they returned home, she was wide awake and paced the hallway outside their bedroom, picking at her bandage and examining her hand as though it were a foreign object. Jake tried several times to get her to lie down, but each time she threw the covers off, climbed out of bed, and began pacing again. Finally Jake gave up trying to get any sleep himself. The sun would be up in an hour anyway.

He took Ellen's hand and led her into the kitchen. There, as gently as though she could understand every word, he told her what he had decided to do.

"Ellen, I want to tell you something, honey." He hadn't used the endearment for so long that it sounded alien to him. "In just a few days we're going to take you to a beautiful place called Parkside Manor. They'll take good care of you there, Ellen." A sob rose in his throat as the reality of his decision sank in. They were sitting across the table from each other, and with a detached expression, Ellen looked at Jake and leaned into his hand as he stroked her cheek.

"I can't do it anymore, El. I can't take care of you as you deserve to be cared for. But they have nurses and doctors there who can help you. They won't ever let you get lost or get hurt like you do here." He was crying openly now. "I'll come and visit you every day, El. And we can still go for our walks in the evening. But you can't stay here anymore. . . . You just can't."

Ellen stared at him, looking straight into his eyes—a rare thing. Then she reached up, and with her bandaged hand, gently wiped a tear from his cheek.

"Hurts . . . oh . . . oh . . . oh . . . hurts. Hurts! Away . . . away . . . away. Go away. No . . . no . . . no . . . Away . . . away . . . away . . . away . . . away. . . ." Ellen's words were spoken in the lifeless, sing-song voice that Alzheimer's had given her, but the words themselves were poignant, and with pain Jake realized that they came from her heart.

Jake made the arrangements with Parkside and set the date for Ellen to move in. He called each of the kids and gently told them what he had decided to do. Brant and Kyle were upset. They hadn't realized Jake was considering such a drastic solution, but they seemed to understand their father's decision, and each in his own way gave Jake his approval.

Jana was silent when Jake told her. He tried to elicit a response from her, but she gave him a frosty "thank you for calling," and all but hung up on him. Jake heard the tears in her voice and knew it was more anguish than anger. He decided to give the news time to soak in before he tried to make peace with her and convince her that he was doing the right thing. But he was upset at having Jana angry with him, and it ate at him all day. Making this decision was hard enough without having his children turn against him. He felt enough guilt as it was. Couldn't they understand that?

He came home from work two days later and found a letter in the mail from Jana. He opened it, and the accusing words in Jana's precise, rounded scroll stung him. He sat down and rested his forehead heavily on the palm of his hand.

Dear Dad,

This is the most difficult letter I have ever written. You are my dad and I love and respect you. I want you to know that comes above everything else I am about to say, but my heart is broken by what you have decided to do. I'm sorry, but I don't understand how you can put my mother in a nursing home. I know, Dad, that these last few years have been very hard on you, and I know Mom has been getting worse and worse, but still, there has to be another solution. Honest, Dad, if she were seventy or eighty years old I could understand it, but she's only just fifty! I feel like it will literally kill her to be thrown in there with all those old people.

No—I feel like Mom has already died. How will our family ever be the same without Mom at the house? I know you say we will bring her home for holidays and for visits, but it won't be the same. Do you just throw away someone you love because it gets a little inconvenient?

Dad, you know I've offered to quit my job and come and help with Mom. I can't understand why you won't accept my help. Mark promised he would support me if that is what I decide to do. Will you please reconsider? Dad, I've never begged for anything in my life, but I am begging you to change your mind. I don't know what else I can say.

I will love you no matter what you decide, but I'm not sure I can ever forgive you for this. I'm just being honest.

Love,

Jana

P.S. I do love you, Dad. Please know that!

Jake was deeply hurt by Jana's letter. Her postscript did little to soften the blows she had dealt with her harsh words. Yet Jake knew in his heart the decision he had made was right and best for everyone. It wasn't ideal, but there was no other solution. He knew Ellen would never have wanted Jana to leave her husband for her sake. And he also knew Jana didn't have a true picture of how bad things had become with Ellen.

He had tried to be honest with the kids. Since the Thanksgiving when Kyle and Brant had been so upset about Ellen's deterioration, he had been careful to warn them of any new developments in her health. But unless one lived with Alzheimer's day in and day out, there was no way to really understand the horror of it. And the father in Jake wanted to spare his children the uglier details of their mother's decline. He couldn't bring himself to tell them that Ellen had occasionally begun to be incontinent; or that she nearly had to be spoon-fed now. He felt bound to preserve some of Ellen's dignity.

Twice he started a reply to Jana's letter, but the words he could think to write seemed sterile and uncaring on paper. Finally he picked up the phone and called her.

"Jana, it's Dad. Please don't say anything until I finish what I have to tell you, and then we'll talk."

"I'm listening." Was there contrition in her voice?

"Jana, I really do understand how upset you are. And I don't blame you, honey. But you need to know that I have looked at all the alternatives. I spent an entire week writing lists of options and making phone calls trying to find a way to keep Mom at home. There just isn't any way to make it work, honey. I can't keep my job and take care of Mom too, and if I lose my job, I can't afford any kind of help for Mom.

"Jana, I appreciate your offer and Mom would have too—I know you made it out of love. But I also know that she would never have allowed it. You belong with Mark. Mom would have absolutely hated the thought of her sickness causing you two to separate or of putting that kind of strain on your marriage.

"I don't want to sound cruel, Jana, but Mom has reached the point where I don't think it's going to make much difference where she lives. As long as we go see her, and as long as she is being taken care of, I think she's as happy as she'll ever be. And it'll be a lot easier once she gets a private room. Then we can have some privacy when we visit her."

It was silent on Jana's end, so he continued. "I appreciate your honesty. I really do. I'm glad you let me know how you are feeling, but I want you to understand that I haven't made this decision selfishly. I've thought and prayed about this long and hard, and I truly feel this is the best thing we can do for Mom right now. I don't know any other way, honey."

For a long time Jana was silent, and Jake didn't try to fill the void with more reasoning. He had said all he could. Finally, he said simply, "Jana, I'm just asking you to trust me, and if you still think I'm wrong, to forgive me. Do you think you can do that?" Jake heard Jana give a big sigh and then begin to cry. Her voice breaking, she said, "Oh, of course I forgive you, Dad. And I do trust you. I'm not sure I understand all your reasons, but I trust you. I know you want what's best for Mom too." She paused, then sheepishly added, "I'm sorry about the letter. I wish I could take it back. Can you . . . can you forgive me?"

"You didn't do anything wrong, honey. You were just being honest. It's okay."

"Thanks, Dad. I love you."

"I love you too, honey. We'll see you next week, okay?"

Her sobs started anew, but through her tears she managed to tell him goodbye.

He hung up the phone, grateful for a quick reconciliation. He knew it might take some time for Jana to work through her resentments, but he needed everyone behind him to go through with this.

———— ∞ ————

Too soon the day arrived to take Ellen to Parkside. The kids wanted to be there. None of them were happy about Jake's decision, but they were supporting him, and they wanted to help.

Until Ellen got a private room, there was nothing to take except her clothes and a few personal items. Jake really didn't need the help, but he let his children come anyway, and he was grateful for their company.

They gathered at the house early on a Monday morning. Jake had already packed the clothes and toiletries Ellen would need. Jana went through the motions of looking through her mother's closets and drawers, but the only thing she added to the items Jake had already packed was the little porcelain bluebird she had given her mother for Christmas. When Jana was small, Ellen had given her the coveted privilege of helping dust the collection of fragile little birds. Jake thought to offer the collection to Jana, but it seemed too morbid for a day already fraught with finality.

The boys put the two small bags in the trunk of Jake's car, and Jana helped Ellen into the passenger seat beside Jake. Then, with the three kids in the backseat, they began the short drive to Parkside.

As Jake backed out of the driveway, he glanced in the rearview mirror. Reflected there, like ghosts from the past, were his three children—Jana, with a brother on each side— just the way it had been for so many years. His family, all piled in the car together, appeared to be off for a day of adventure. Who would have thought it would end like this? He swallowed the lump that lodged in his throat and tried to concentrate on the road in front of him.

The nurses had Ellen settled in less than twenty minutes. She sat in the chair by her window and stared outside. The room was large and bright, but it had the feel of a hospital room. A curtain divided the two halves of the room, and the beds were bulky and institutional. There were only two other pieces of furniture in her area: a small bedside table, and a chair upholstered in leatherlike vinyl. Jake spread a favorite afghan of Ellen's—one MaryEllen had crocheted—across the foot of her bed and hung her bathrobe on a hook near the closet. Jana put the little bird on the windowsill in front of Ellen. Unfortunately, these additions did little to make the room seem like home.

Ellen's window looked onto the crowded parking lot, but she didn't seem to mind the view, and Jake was grateful that at least she had something to look at besides the stark interior of her room.

Jake and the kids stood awkwardly around her chair. Did she understand what was happening? Jake would have given anything to know her thoughts, just for that moment. But her eyes gave nothing away, and her voice had long been silenced of any language that Jake could comprehend.

Ellen's roommate was a sweet woman in her eighties. Like the other residents on this wing, she had Alzheimer's. Ellen was assigned the bed by the far wall, so they had to walk through Stella's half of the room to get to Ellen's side. Stella had a friendly smile for them each time they walked through, but she also had something to say to each one, and none of them could make sense of her disjointed comments. It was awkward and embarrassing.

When they had stayed for an uncomfortable half hour, Jake kissed Ellen goodbye and casually told her that he would see her tomorrow. The kids followed his lead and gave her farewell hugs. Ellen seemed oblivious to her new surroundings, and she made no reply to their goodbyes.

Brant and Kyle had to get back to Urbana early in the evening, but Jake took Jana out for pizza before she headed for Chicago. They talked about Jana's job and about the weather, carefully avoiding the one thing that was foremost in both their minds. It was an uneasy, painful time, and Jake was relieved when the waiter brought the check.

Jake invited Jana to the house, but she made excuses and started back to the city, saying her goodbyes in the driveway. Though Jana was making an effort to be supportive of Jake's decision, he sensed that she still felt some resentment toward him. And he understood that it was simply too difficult for her to go back into the empty house now.

He expected it to be hard for him too. He parked the car in the garage and went in through the kitchen. The house looked the same. He walked down the hallway to their bedroom, testing his emotions. Ellen's bedside table was empty except for the alarm clock that he had decided she wouldn't need. Other than that, nothing was different in here either. Since that cold night when he had moved their bedroom down from the attic, he had felt like a stranger in his own home.

Jake waited all evening for the impact to hit him. For the guilt to overwhelm him. For the sadness to creep in. But all he felt was relief.

Ellen was safe. He could sleep in peace tonight for the first time in many months, knowing that she was being well cared for. He had made the most difficult decision of his life and was convinced he had done what was best for everyone. Tomorrow evening he would take flowers to his wife, and together they would walk a new path.

9

Julia Sinclair stood at the kitchen counter up to her elbows in the sticky bread dough she was kneading. Little clouds of flour puffed out with each turn of the lump, dusting Julia's sweatshirt with a fine white powder. The phone rang from the den, and with a groan she hurriedly wiped her hands on a dish towel as she raced to beat the answering machine.

"Hello. Sinclair residence."

"Yes, Julia Sinclair, please."

"This is Julia," she said cautiously and thinking to herself, *So help me, if this is another sales call, I'll scream.* She had been interrupted twice in the space of an hour, and her patience was growing thin.

"Yes, Ms. Sinclair. This is Paul Cravens at Parkside Manor. You submitted an application a few weeks ago. . . ?" His voice trailed off in a question. "I apologize that it's taken so long to get back to you. I guess I should ask you first of all if you're still interested in the job?"

Julia had mailed the application almost two months ago

and had given up on getting even a negative response. But, yes. Yes, she was very interested. She told him so.

"Good, good. Well, I must say we were very impressed with your resumé, and we'd like to set up an appointment for an interview. We do have a couple other people we are considering for the job, but those interviews haven't been scheduled yet, so the calendar is pretty wide open."

They agreed on the following Monday morning, and Julia quickly arranged to get the morning off work. She had been up-front with her boss about this job search. She liked her accounting job at the small medical clinic, but she became more determined each day to get the boys out of the city.

The school year was quickly coming to a close, and a sobering look at her financial state had decreed that the boys could not go back next year to the private school they now attended. Martin's insurance had been generous, but Julia was painfully aware that the funds would have to stretch over many years—until the boys were on their own. College expenses alone were going to kill her, but they still had many years of schooling to face before that. To her, it was unthinkable to throw the boys into public school in this city after their sheltered years at St. Mark's.

She had applied for jobs in several small towns in the surrounding communities, but so far nothing had panned out. The prospect of this job and the small-town life that would accompany it filled her with optimism. It was so good to be looking forward to something instead of looking back.

She returned to her kneading, mindlessly forming the fragrant loaves while her thoughts delighted in the possibilities ahead, and her voice whispered a prayer of hope.

<hr />

Julia hurriedly parked the car, gathered her purse and tote bag from the seat beside her, and on wobbling high heels ran toward the door of Springhill Medical Clinic. Of all the days to oversleep!

It was her last day of work at Springhill, and she met it with ambivalent feelings. She had loved this job. Some of her closest friendships had begun in this office. Of course she would keep in touch with her friends here—Calypso wasn't that far from Chicago—but she knew things would never quite be the same. Without the bond of working in the same environment, without the shared problems of the workplace, it was inevitable that friendships would change and perhaps even fade.

Julia would have dreaded this day had she not been so excited about the new job awaiting her in Calypso. She was thriving on the exhilarating independence she felt in making this decision for herself and Sam and Andy. The boys' lack of enthusiasm tempered her own a bit, but she knew they were young and would adjust quickly. She honestly felt this move would do all of them a world of good. It was time for a change.

She hung her jacket in the cloakroom and opened the door to the accounting office.

"Surprise! Surprise!"

The room was filled with streamers and balloons, and a computer banner spanned one wall, declaring, *"We'll miss you, Julia! Best wishes on the new job!"*

Tears came quickly to her eyes. The faces of these people she loved like family smiled liquidly before her. She grinned through her tears, at first embarrassed by her show of emotion, then suddenly unconcerned if they saw her break down.

There were hugs all around, and Julia was led to a table laden with cakes, punch, and a beautifully wrapped gift.

Julia was overwhelmed. She had never considered they might do something like this for her.

"Oh, you guys! I can't believe this." Her voice grew stronger as she began teasing them about all the fuss they had made over her. "Mindy Durham, did you have anything to do with this?"

"Wouldn't you like to know?" But Mindy's grin told the truth.

"You sneaky little thing, you. I didn't have a *clue*! I can't believe you pulled this off!"

The emotion of the moment gave way to jovial laughter, joking, and the warm camaraderie of friends in the work-place.

Over cake and coffee they presented Julia with the gift. She slid the lamé bow off and ran her fingers gently under the seam of the gilded wrapping paper, being careful not to crush it. "Ooh, this is almost too pretty to unwrap." The paper fell away to reveal a thick white box, which Julia opened with candid curiosity.

Inside was the oak mantel clock that Julia had yearned for ever since she saw it displayed in the window of an exclusive gift shop down the street from the clinic.

Julia gasped and the tears started anew. "Oh! Oh, it's beautiful. I've wanted this so badly! But . . . how did you know?"

Then she recalled that several of her co-workers had seen her admiring the clock when they walked by the shop together after lunch one day. Julia noticed a card attached to the back of the clock, and she opened it and read the blurring words of the inscription. *"To Julia . . . A Time For Everything."*

Though the lump in her throat kept her from speaking for a minute, the emotion she felt was warm and uplifting. It had been the most difficult year of her life, yet through it all she had been taken care of. She knew it was the hand of God that had carried her through the valley of grief, but she marveled that He had done it in such a tangible way— through the arms of her parents, the joy of her sons, the perfect fitting together of circumstances, and now through the love of these friends who surrounded her. She felt her faith swelling in slow motion, as though she were witnessing the unfolding of a flower through a time-lapse lens.

In the days and weeks following Martin's death, she had struggled to see a speck of truth in the biblical promise that "all things work together for good." Now the meaning of those words was coming into focus, clearer and sharper each moment, and she felt blessed beyond imagining that the promise was for *her*.

She spent the rest of the day relishing precious last moments with her friends. When she cleaned out her desk that afternoon, her sadness was diffused by a sense of gratitude, purpose, and joyful anticipation for the future.

10

For Jake Brighton, the weeks filed by like marching soldiers, and life settled into a neat, cheerless routine. He came home from work each evening and changed clothes. Then he went to Parkside, usually arriving just in time to walk Ellen back from the dining room.

Occasionally he brought Chinese takeout to her room and ate there with her for old times' sake. The China Garden had closed down years ago. The restaurant had changed ownership several times over twenty years, and the food never was as good as it had been when it was "their" restaurant. Ellen had actually shed tears that long-ago afternoon when they drove by and saw the boarded windows and the "Closed" signs plastered across the doors of their old haunt. Still, now and then through the years they had ordered egg foo yong at a new Chinese place, just for tradition's sake. Now Jake made a feeble effort to continue the habit. He didn't think Ellen remembered the significance of the feast he brought, but somehow, it comforted him to keep alive a tradition from happier days.

Only two months after Ellen moved into Parkside, a private room became available. The room was large and full of light, with a view of the residents' enclosed courtyard. The walls were papered in a soft shade of yellow, and the draperies were a cheerful floral. Much effort had been made to avoid an institutional look. It was a huge improvement over the sterile shared room, and Jake felt incredibly fortunate that a private room had become available so quickly.

At first he was grateful mostly for the kids' sakes, for they were happy and relieved. But after Ellen was settled in the new room, and they had brought in some furniture, paintings, and the rest of Ellen's little collection of porcelain birds, Jake realized how much easier his visits had become. He could bring a book, lounge on the couch, and read. He didn't have Stella to deal with; he didn't feel as though he were in a fishbowl with everyone watching to see how he was handling all this. His time with Ellen felt more like companionship now that her room felt more like home.

They walked together nearly every night. When the weather was warm, they went outside and strolled the sidewalks on the grounds. When it was chilly, they walked the long corridors inside the building. Ellen was having more and more trouble getting around, her steps a funny little uneven shuffle. But her doctors said she should continue to walk as much and as often as possible. So Jake tried not to miss, except for the nights he had school board meetings or other obligations.

After spending an hour or so at Parkside, Jake usually went straight home, fixed a light supper, and then read or watched TV until the news was over. His last thought before sleep overtook him each night was that he would wake to a day no different than this one had been.

Jake tried not to dwell on his circumstances. He tried not to feel sorry for himself. But it wasn't easy. He was starved for companionship, hungry for conversation.

Except for Rob Anderson, the high school principal and a close friend, Jake had no one at all to whom he could really talk. Rob was a godsend—a good listener, a respected source of advice, and one of the few people in Calypso who could beat Jake at tennis. But Rob had his own family and the busy life they brought. Jake tried not to burden him too often. Sometimes it just felt good to play a challenging game of tennis and talk about nothing more than the weather or the football game the night before.

Jake's job became his lifeline. He wasn't sure he would have survived the loneliness without it.

⎯⎯∝⎯⎯

One morning late in July, Jake arrived at the office to find that his secretary had scheduled an early appointment for him. Barbara seldom made appointments without checking with Jake first, so he was curious who could have business so urgent that they had managed to persuade Barbara to change her policy.

"I apologize, Mr. Brighton. I told the woman you may not be in, but she was very insistent that she see you right away. I hope there's no conflict."

"No problem, Barbara. Did she say what she wanted?"

"Well, something about transferring her kids to Calypso schools. I believe the family is moving here from the city. I told her she needed to file the applications with the principals, but she insisted that she speak to you personally. She was very persuasive."

Jake was amused, for Barbara wasn't easily persuaded. He hid a grin. "I see. Well, I have to run over to the high school for a few minutes, but I should be back by eight-thirty or so. It shouldn't be a problem."

When Jake got back, the door to his office was open, and he saw someone was waiting in the upholstered chair in front of his desk. He cleared his throat to announce his arrival and shrugged out of his suit jacket, hanging it on the hook behind his door.

The woman fumbled with the purse in her lap and started to stand, but Jake motioned her to keep her seat. He extended his right hand.

"Hello there. Sorry to keep you waiting. I'm Jake Brighton."

"Hello. Julia Sinclair."

"Good to meet you. How can I help you, Mrs. Sinclair?"

"Julia, please."

She had a warm handshake and a friendly smile. She spoke in a low, melodious voice. He guessed her to be in her mid-thirties, and while she wasn't classically beautiful, there was an aura of confidence and poise about her that was very striking. She was simply but stylishly dressed in a pale blue skirt and blouse. Her honey-colored hair was pulled into a smooth chignon. She wore no jewelry save for a simple gold band on her left ring finger. This Jake noticed when she began to speak, because she spoke with her hands. Her fingers were long and slender, and her hands were as expressive as some women's eyes.

"Well, Julia, what can I do for you? My secretary tells me you're moving here from Chicago?"

"Well, we hope to. That's why I wanted to talk to you personally. I realize that enrollment usually goes through the principals, and I apologize for taking your time about this, but you see, we'll be in two different schools here, and I want to be certain we can get enrolled in the district even though we're not officially residents yet. I've just started working at Parkside Manor—I'm an accountant there—and we do plan to move to Calypso as soon as possible. Unfortunately, there's no guarantee we'll have found a place to live by the time school starts."

The reference to Parkside startled Jake, and he struggled to concentrate on what she was saying.

"I've just started house hunting. My two sons have been attending a private school in Chicago, but I would like them to be able to start school here in the fall. Sam will be a sophomore and Andy an eighth grader. I really hope we'll be moved by then, but there aren't many houses on the market here right now."

"That's for sure. We've had so many people moving into Calypso recently. Your husband's job is in Chicago?" he asked.

"Oh, I'm sorry. I should have explained. My husband died . . . um . . . it will be a year ago in October. It's just the boys and me." Julia swallowed hard. Her grief was obviously still fresh.

"Oh, I'm so sorry."

"Martin was killed in a car accident. It's been a pretty tough year." She swallowed again, struggling to keep back tears. "It's been especially rough on Andy—my eighth grader—but we're managing okay now. I want to get the boys out of the city. I can't afford the private school any longer, and I just can't bear to put them in public school in the city. They've never known anything but small classrooms and a private school setting. I feel very fortunate to have found this job at Parkside. It's a really nice place, and they've been very understanding of my problems with the commute and the boys' schedules."

Jake could have reaffirmed her praise of the facility, mentioning his connection to Parkside. But he found himself drawing back—dodging the subject. *Why?* he asked himself. Amazingly, this was the first time he'd been faced with an opening for explaining his situation to a stranger. Was he ashamed of Ellen?

He fought to focus on the woman's words.

"So, what do I need to do to get the boys enrolled for next fall?" she asked.

Jake cleared his throat and forced himself to concentrate. He tried to answer her question.

"Well, assuming you find a house, just show up for enrollment next month. I'll send you a schedule as soon as the dates are set. Unfortunately, we do have a large number of requests for out-of-district enrollments, and with the influx of new people we've had into town, enrollment is up anyway. So just in case you haven't moved by then, we'll get your name on a waiting list. Of course, you're at an advantage getting your name in early, and we'll definitely take into consideration your plans to move here and your employment here.

"If I can brag a bit, Calypso is reputed to be one of the best school districts in the state. My three children all graduated from CHS, and from a parent's point of view, I can't say enough good things about this district.

"We'll have you fill out an application here today, which we will file with the school principals. Then after the regular enrollment is tabulated, the board will decide how many out-of-district applications to accept. Unfortunately, that cuts it pretty close for those who are rejected. Um . . . if you could possibly find housing in the district—even just a rental—that would guarantee the boys' enrollment. In the meantime, we'll see what we can do. I think we can probably work something out."

Julia filled out the necessary forms, chatting amiably with Jake as she wrote. Her eyes sparkled when she spoke, in spite of the sadness that hid behind them. When she left, Jake felt a disquieting mixture of emotions. He felt a strange elation at meeting this warm, candid woman. It had been a long time since he'd had a pleasant conversation with a woman who wasn't expressing sympathy for him over Ellen. He realized that pity, though well intentioned, was cloying. It was refreshing to relate to someone without the specter of his tragedy coloring the exchange.

And yet, Jake felt guilty that he had been so reluctant to mention Ellen. He knew he had consciously avoided any mention of her, when under other circumstances, her name would have come up several times. This unremarkable encounter with Julia Sinclair had been strangely unsettling.

⚬⚬⚬

When Jake got home that evening there was a message on the answering machine from Brant. His voice had a hint of urgency in it, though his message was nonchalant.

"Hey, Dad. Brant. Uh, give me a call when you can. I've got to work tonight, but I should be back by nine or so. Catch you later."

At nine-fifteen Jake dialed Brant's number.

He answered on the first ring.

"Hi, Brant. What's up?"

"Dad! What's up? Well, quite a bit, actually."

He sounded embarrassed. Jake could almost hear him squirm.

Finally Brant blurted, "What would you think if I told you Cynthia and I are going to get married?"

"Are you serious? When?" Jake was incredulous. He hadn't expected this.

"Well, we're talking about this winter. Cynthia has always wanted a winter wedding. And, well . . ." He launched into what sounded like a well-rehearsed speech. "I know it will be hard when Cynthia has so much school left. I'd probably have to get a second job, and I know money would be tight, but . . . well, we think it will be easier if we're married and not using up so much energy thinking about each other all the time and trying to get together. We think we can make it work." He paused and caught his breath. "You have any opinions on that?"

"I sure do. I think . . ." Jake tried to sound stern and paused for effect. Then with a smile in his voice, he said, "I think you're absolutely right. You two have gone together for a long time, and I know you wouldn't make a decision like this without thinking it over carefully. Brant, I'm really happy for you."

He could hear Brant's relief on the other end.

"I'll have to tell you, son, the first time you brought Cynthia home, your mom and I told each other we hoped you wouldn't let her get away. She's like family already."

"You really think so?"

"You know I do. You two certainly have my blessing, Brant."

"Thanks, Dad. Dad?" Brant's voice broke. "Do you think Mom . . . do you think she should come to the wedding?"

"Oh, Brant." Jake sighed heavily. "It's up to you and Cynthia, but I'm afraid it would be hard for everybody. Mom doesn't know anyone these days. Lately, I don't think she even comprehends that I'm there. You know Mom would have given you and Cynthia her blessing before she got sick. She'll be with us in spirit no matter what you decide."

"Thanks, Dad."

"Hey, you tell Cynthia congratulations. I'm very happy for you two."

Midmorning, on the tenth of August, a large moving van pulled up to the curb of the apartment building at Lakeview. Sam Sinclair, who had stood sentry at the front window all morning, announced its arrival with a shout.

"Mom! They're here."

"Okay, let's get busy," she hollered down the hallway. "Andy?"

"I'm in my room. . . ."

"Hey . . . let's go. They're here."

"Okay, okay, I'm coming." His tone was surly, and he slammed his bedroom door defiantly behind him. Andy was dragging his heels about the move. His father's death had changed everything, and he was angry that he was being torn from his friends and the only home he had ever known. He plodded reluctantly down the hallway to get his "marching orders."

Julia ignored his rudeness and mustered a cheerful grin. "Ready?" She didn't wait for an answer. "Okay. You and Sam start closing up those boxes in the kitchen—use the packing tape and make sure they're secure—and I'll find out which room the movers want to haul out first."

They worked steadily through the morning, and by noon the apartment was empty, and the van was on its way to Calypso. Julia loaded her houseplants and a small box of fragile items into the back of the car. While the boys vied for space in the cramped backseat, Julia walked through the rooms to be sure they hadn't left anything behind.

Her heels clicked on the bare wood floors and echoed through the hollow rooms of the apartment. It was an effort to remain matter-of-fact about this final walk through the old apartment that had been her home for a dozen years. These rooms held so many memories.

She walked into Andy's bedroom, and through eyes moist with remembrance, she saw it, not as the recent haven of an almost-teenager, but as the nursery it had been twelve years ago. She and Martin had brought Andrew David Sinclair home from the hospital to this room. She could still see the cloud blue curtains at the window and hear the plinking metallic notes of his little clown-shaped music box. *"Where are the clowns? Send in the clowns? There ought to be clowns."* The tune sang over and over in her mind, and she longed to hold in her arms the chubby infant it had soothed. She closed the door silently and walked down the hallway.

She poked her head into Sam's room and the master bedroom, and, seeing both were empty, closed the doors. It was not their bedroom that evoked memories of Martin. It was the bathroom. A large old-fashioned room, she had always loved its pedestal sink and deep, footed tub. A clerestory window let in sunlight that showed off the rich patina of the dark oak wainscoting. How many mornings had she leaned against this doorframe—a thick terry bathrobe wrapped snugly around her, her hands warmed by a steaming mug of coffee—watching Martin shave? She had never grown tired of watching his ritual. It was the one time she had him captive . . . his lips silenced by a thick lather of shaving cream, the boys still asleep in their beds, and the phone quiet in the early morning. It had been her favorite time of day, and she realized that since his death she had not once thought of it until today.

She closed the bathroom door. It was hard to say goodbye to this home—to turn the final pages of the story she and Martin had written together.

The blast of the car horn shook her back to the present . . . to reality. She didn't know how long she had been standing here, but the boys were growing impatient, and it was time to be on the road.

∞

Jake was shopping for groceries on a sultry evening in August when he rounded a corner by the produce and nearly had a head-on collision with Julia Sinclair. She was dressed casually in jeans and a sweatshirt, and her hair was pulled into a sloppy ponytail. Her grocery cart was piled almost to overflowing.

"Well, hi there," Jake said when he recognized her.

"Oh, hi."

"Does this huge mound of groceries mean that you're an official Calypso resident now?" he teased.

"As a matter of fact, it does. We just finished moving the last load from the city yesterday, and the house looks like a tornado went through it. We've got stuff sitting all over the house in boxes, but growing boys have to be fed whether the kitchen's in order or not."

"How well I remember. We couldn't keep enough food in the fridge when our kids were that age. So, you found a house, then?"

"Yes." She was beaming. "Do you know where Sweetbriar Lane is?"

"Isn't that just south of Broadway?"

"Yes. Our house is on the far east end of Sweetbriar, in a nice neighborhood. I think I really got a good deal. It's a two-story with a double garage, so we have lots of room. And the boys are thrilled because there's a basketball backboard and hoop in the driveway. They weren't too happy about leaving all their friends in the city, but they've already made friends in our neighborhood. I think we're going to love small-town life." Her enthusiasm was contagious.

"That's great. Well, welcome to Calypso. We're gearing up for enrollment on the tenth. Did you get the information from our office?"

"To tell you the truth, I haven't looked at the mail for two days. We had a stack a mile high at the post office this morning, and I haven't sorted through it yet, but it's probably in there somewhere."

"Well, if you don't find it, just give the district office a call, and we'll get something in the mail to you. Boy, it doesn't seem possible that school will be starting in a couple of weeks. This summer has sure flown by."

"Tell me about it. I just hope we're settled in before school starts."

They stood in the aisle, cart to cart, and visited for twenty minutes. Their conversation came easily, and Jake had the impression she was flirting with him. He was guiltily afraid that he was reciprocating.

When she discovered the ice cream melting in her cart, she bid him farewell.

"Well, I'd better get home and feed the troops. Nice to see you again."

"You too. I'm glad you found a house. Good luck with the settling."

They waved and headed in opposite directions. Again, Jake felt that uncomfortable mix of emotions—boyish anticipation at the possibility of seeing her again, and a stirring of guilt that he had enjoyed their encounter so much. He finished his shopping and went home to put the groceries away.

All evening long, images of an attractive honey-haired woman flitted through his mind as he replayed their conversation over and over. He felt like a silly teenager with a first-time crush on a girl. "This is ridiculous," he said aloud and willed himself to think about something else. But ten minutes later he was thinking of her again.

He went to bed that night more acutely aware than ever of just how lonely he was.

The next few weeks were busy for Jake. School started and with it all the headaches of getting the term running smoothly. There were some curriculum changes that weren't working out as well as he had hoped, and a high school English teacher had a heart attack the second day of school and was under doctor's orders to lay off work for at least six weeks. It was early in October before Jake felt as though things were on an even keel, and he could cut back to regular hours and relax a bit.

Jake found himself volunteering to help in the press box at the high school football games simply so he could feel justified in attending the games. He feared what people would think seeing him enjoying himself at a ball game. Though he knew probably no one judged him more harshly than he did himself, he still felt guilty for allowing himself even the smallest pleasure when Ellen was so bereft of any.

He had not played tennis or jogged since late July, and the bathroom scale was starting to creep up at an alarming rate. He knew he should be more careful how he ate, too. Ellen had always been adamant about having plenty of fresh vegetables and fruit in their diet. She had scolded Jake if he hit the doughnut shop too often in the mornings. Now he found himself grabbing fast food several times a week because it was too much trouble to cook for one. It was all starting to catch up with him, and he resolved he would make time to get out and exercise now that things had settled down at school.

He came home from work and changed into shorts and a sweatshirt. The temperatures were still in the sixties during the day, but the evening air was cool—perfect for jogging. He headed out the back door feeling proud of himself for finally taking the initiative to get out and run.

It felt great to be outdoors. Jake ran at a brisk pace for the first half-mile, but then he felt the long hiatus from exercise catching up with him. By the end of the first mile, he was out of breath and sweating profusely in spite of the brisk air. He slowed to a walk.

He had run from Oaklawn to the large park where he and Rob played tennis. There was a jogging path that ran the circumference of the park, and if he circled this twice, he would have his four miles in by the time he jogged back home. He broke back into a slow run, embarrassed to be so winded after such a short time.

As he started his second jaunt around the track, he came up behind a woman in blue shorts and a hooded sweatshirt. She moved to the side of the narrow track so he could pass. He turned around, still at a jog, to acknowledge her courtesy.

"Mr. Brighton!" It was Julia Sinclair's voice.

"Oh, hi!" He slowed down to match her pace and pointed to her covered head. "I almost didn't recognize you with the hood. Hey, call me Jake, please. I don't feel like Mr. Brighton on the jogging track. Especially when I'm about to keel over." He rolled his eyes and clutched his throat with an exaggerated gagging sound.

She laughed. "To tell you the truth," she admitted sheepishly, "I couldn't remember your first name . . . Jake. You must hate running as much as I do."

"Well, if I hadn't let myself get so out of shape, I would probably be enjoying this. But it's been weeks since I did anything remotely athletic."

"Me too. It really ticks me off how quickly I can get out of shape if I don't keep at it. Is this where you always run?"

"Oh, I try to keep it interesting and go someplace different once in a while. I like to run here because I don't have to fight the traffic, and I can keep track of how far I've gone. I don't know why it really matters, but somehow I feel better if I can come home and say I ran four miles or five miles or whatever."

"Wow. Do you always run that far?"

"Well, I try to. I figure as long as I'm out here anyway, I may as well make it worth my time."

She rolled her eyes. "I'm doing well if I make it two or three."

Jake shrugged. "Hey, at least you're running."

"Well, I'm probably slowing you down."

"No . . . I'm going about as fast as my lungs will let me right now." He didn't want her to get away. He scrambled to think of something to say . . . to keep the conversation going.

"So how are the boys liking school by now?"

"Oh, it's going well. Sam is having a blast playing football. He kind of hated those early-morning practices the first couple weeks, but the games make it all worthwhile."

"He's got some talent. I don't get to very many of the junior varsity games, but I saw him play against Hanover and he looked great. He's really got speed. Has he gotten to play quite a bit?"

She beamed proudly. "He started the last two games. He's thrilled about that. He's already planning a big career with the Bears." She laughed, then cringed. "He'd kill me if he knew I told you that."

"My lips are sealed." Julia was getting winded, so Jake slowed to a fast walk. "So how about Andy? Is everything going all right for him, too?"

Julia sighed. "He's doing okay. Everything is always harder for Andy. I don't know if it's adolescence or if it's just his personality. He seems to take everything so seriously."

"Some kids are made that way."

"Yes, but Andy was always happy-go-lucky before Mar—before his dad died. Sometimes I feel like that accident robbed me of more than a husband." She had a faraway look in her eyes. Suddenly, she remembered herself. "I'm sorry, Jake. You don't want to hear all this."

"No . . . no, that's okay. If there's anything I can do to make things easier for Andy, I want to know. I really do appreciate you sharing this with me. If you don't have any objections, I'll make his teachers aware of the situation. They might have some insights to offer."

"Thank you." Her voice was sweetly sincere. "I didn't mean to put this on you. I know that's not at all a part of your job."

"Hey, I've always felt like anything that affects the kids is my job. I taught for quite a few years before I became superintendent, and I have to say that one of the things I miss about teaching is that intimate contact with the kids."

"Jake, I appreciate that. I'm doing double the worrying about the kids now that I'm both Mom and Dad. Given time, Andy will be okay. He's already made a couple of friends in our neighborhood. It's just that he doesn't feel like he fits in at school yet. But if eighth grade is still anything like it was thirty-some years ago, *nobody* thinks they fit in."

He did some quick math. "If it was thirty years ago, you must have been about five years old in eighth grade." He was fishing brazenly.

She smiled. "I'm forty-three, Jake. I don't mind telling my age."

"I'm sorry. That was a pretty obvious hint, wasn't it? Well, you don't look as though you could be thirty, let alone have been in eighth grade thirty years ago."

She blushed. "Well, thank you. I appreciate the compliment."

They jogged side by side in companionable silence until they came to the park benches at the end of the path. They sat down and talked for another hour, and Jake realized afresh how much he missed this easy, familiar conversation. He had accepted the silence in his life because he had no choice, but now he felt years of suppressed thoughts and emotions welling within him, begging for expression. He felt he could talk to her forever.

Jake came home and showered, whistling all the while.

That fresh air did me a world of good, he thought to himself. *I need to run more often.*

Jake dressed and drove to Parkside. Ellen was still in the dining room when he arrived. The evening meal was served at exactly five-thirty at Parkside, and Jake rarely arrived in time to share supper with her. Tonight the table where she sat was crowded, so he kissed her on the cheek and told her he would come back for her when she was finished eating. She looked up at his face, but her expression did not acknowledge him.

Jake went down the hallway to her room. He threw out a wilted bunch of chrysanthemums that he had brought from the garden at home the week before. He rinsed the vase and set it on the bathroom counter to dry and made a mental note to bring another bouquet when he came tomorrow.

He straightened the books on her night table. He was fairly certain that Ellen had lost her ability to read, but he continued to supply her with a new book every few days, just in case.

Absentmindedly, he leafed through the album of family pictures he had fixed for her. Though Ellen rarely looked at the album, he knew the nurses and Ellen's other caregivers did. He hoped it would give them a sense of who she had been.

He glanced at the clock, and seeing almost ten minutes

had passed, he closed her door behind him and hurried down the hall to the dining room.

Ellen was sitting alone at the table, tapping a fork against her cup. The busboys were clearing the tables, visiting loudly across the room with each other. Jake came up behind Ellen and put his hands on her shoulders.

"Ready to go back to your room, Ellen?" He asked the question as always, expecting no answer in return.

Silently she pushed her chair clumsily away from the table, took his waiting arm, and they walked slowly down the corridor to her room.

Jake spent the next hour beside his wife on the sofa in her room, but his mind was a million miles away in rapt conversation with one Julia Sinclair.

Jake ran into Julia in the park again just a week later. As before, they fell into easy conversation, jogging to the end of the path, then claiming a park bench and talking until the sun disappeared behind the trees and he could find no excuse for staying longer.

They shared many of the same values and philosophies, yet there was an edge to their conversation that gave it an excitement Jake couldn't quite explain. Though he tried to push the comparison from his mind, it reminded him of the stimulating exchanges he and Ellen had always enjoyed. He didn't want to compare Julia to Ellen. It seemed disloyal to Ellen—and unfair to Julia. But he couldn't help it.

It was becoming an effort for Jake to keep the conversation centered on Julia. He walked a precarious tightrope in order not to reveal too much about his situation. He hadn't told Julia about Ellen. He talked with her about his grown children, but he didn't talk about his marital status.

He told himself that he was keeping Ellen a "secret" because he didn't want Julia's sympathy . . . because he didn't want to burden her already heavy heart with *his* woes . . . because he didn't want her to pity him as did virtually everyone else he met. That was part of what drew him to her.

But in the early morning hours, in that unsettled sleep just before awakening, he admitted the truth to himself. He was a liar. He was deceiving her as surely as if he looked squarely into her beautiful eyes and told her a bold-faced lie.

11

The administration offices of Parkside Manor were in the east wing of the sprawling complex. The inside wall of the director's office was actually a huge window that overlooked a residents' lounge and offered a view of the two hallways that forked from the lounge. The accounting offices and the employee entrance, however, were at the back of the building. This was partly a matter of convenience but mostly a matter of security. Every entrance accessible to the residents of Parkside was locked at all times and equipped with a sophisticated alarm system.

As an accountant at Parkside, Julia rarely had contact with the residents or their families. She knew the people the institution served only as names and numbers on a computer print-out. In fact, on the rare occasions she had to walk through the wings of the complex where the residents lived, she was always startled to realize that this was her place of employment. The atmosphere of the accounting department was like that of any other office Julia had worked for—very businesslike, not at all a reflection of the human drama that played out every day on the other side of these walls.

Julia was enjoying her new job immensely. The small-town friendliness that had endeared Calypso to her from the beginning was exemplified by the people who worked in her office. They had made her feel at home here, and it was nice to look forward to work each day. It had been a good decision to move away from Chicago.

Julia loved the house she had bought, and the boys were beginning to feel they belonged to this neighborhood. Yet Chicago was close enough that they could drive in for a visit with old friends and still come home to Calypso the same day. *Home.* It really did feel like home now.

⸙

One evening in November, Julia backed out of her parking space at Parkside. She had worked a bit late trying to catch up on some month-end billing, and now it was almost dark. She turned the car toward the exit, and as she eased past the building, she saw Jake Brighton open the door to the front entrance and disappear inside. He was juggling a large vase of flowers.

"Hmm . . . that's strange. He must have family here," she murmured. "Funny he never mentioned it."

She wondered about it all evening, puzzled at her own curiosity. The next morning while going over some billing statements, she impulsively called up "Brighton" on the computer. There it was. Brighton, Ellen. Room E147. Bill to Jake Brighton, 245 West Oaklawn, Calypso, IL. Jake was paying the bills. It must be someone close to him—his mother or grandmother. Stranger still that he hadn't mentioned it before. She had often spoken of Parkside to Jake.

Julia hadn't admitted, even to herself, how interested

she was in Jake Brighton. But their warm conversations had given her hope that someday she might be able to feel about another man the way she had felt about Martin.

A year after Martin's death, Julia was beginning to come to terms with her grief. It still hurt to be alone, and it was a huge burden to be both mother and father to their boys. But she was beginning to be able to look back on the memories with fondness. In fact, they were beginning to be a comfort to her, rather than a torment. Lately she had begun to reflect on marriage in general and had concluded it was a wonderful institution—one that she would like to enter into again if the right man ever came along.

After her encounter with Jake in the park, Julia had entertained hopes that he might call her and ask her out. She felt as though she may be ready to date. She had purposely jogged in the park, hoping to see Jake again. But when it didn't happen, she reminded herself that she really didn't know much about him at all. She knew he had children because he mentioned them often. Knowing that Julia was a widow, he surely would have said something if he, too, had been widowed, so she assumed he was divorced. He never mentioned his children's mother, and that fact sent up danger signals.

Over her lunch hour, Julia made a rash decision. She felt guilty and a little ridiculous, but nevertheless, she headed down the corridor toward room E147. She didn't have any idea what she would do when she got there, but her curiosity had gotten the better of her.

The door to Ellen Brighton's room was ajar, and Julia could see at first glance that it was a cheery, sunny room. There were vases of flowers on an antique table in front of the window, and the upholstered furniture and botanical prints on the wall gave the room a stylish, yet homey look.

At first, Julia didn't see anyone in the room. Then, just

as she was about to turn and walk back down the hall, the door to the room's private bath creaked open, and a woman with short, dark, curly hair shuffled slowly out. Julia watched her from the doorway, and when the woman turned and sat down in a chair by the window, Julia almost gasped aloud. The noon sunlight illuminated her face, and Julia saw that she was beautiful. She couldn't have been much older than Julia herself. Though she wore no makeup or jewelry, there was a faded elegance about her that was incongruous with this place where she lived. The woman stared out the window, and even from a distance Julia could see the haunted look in her eyes. She was unmistakably a patient here, unmistakably demented, but beautiful nevertheless. What a sad story this must be.

Momentarily, she forgot that the woman had a connection to Jake Brighton. Julia was caught up in the novelty of her youth and her beauty in a place like this. She toyed with the idea of going into the room and speaking with her. But what would she say? She had no business here. She felt mildly ashamed of herself. Her curiosity was gratuitous, bordering on obsessive.

She turned quickly and hurried back to the office. She finished her lunch and got back to work but couldn't keep her mind on the figures before her.

Finally, she called up the Brighton file once again and accessed more information.

Brighton, Ellen . . . Bill to Jake Brighton . . . Occupation: Superintendent of Schools . . . Relationship to patient: husband.

Julia felt as though she had been struck. He was married!

But why should she have assumed otherwise? What a fool she had been. She had imagined he was flirting with her. And—how humiliating—she had flirted with him. Brazenly. She felt herself blush with embarrassment at the very thought of her shameless flirtation. Could she ever face him again?

But *he* hadn't been right in this either. Why hadn't he said that he had a wife? A wife who lived at her very place of employment, for heaven's sake! He had every opportunity to mention it. What was he trying to pull?

"Hang on, Jul," she admonished herself. "It's not like he ever asked you out or anything. You probably just imagined the flirting. You're the one who made a fool of yourself. He didn't owe you his life story." She suddenly felt a horrifying sense of disloyalty to Martin. She was so confused.

She stewed over her discovery all afternoon, and when she got home that night, she was preoccupied and snappish with the boys.

A week passed, and finally, gradually, the obsession lessened. In its place was a vague sense of disappointment. She had to admit, she'd had hopes for Jake Brighton.

"Okay, so life goes on. Get over it, Jul. It's no big deal."

The Calypso Public Library was quieter than usual on a Sunday night in February two hours before closing time. An older couple browsed the stacks, and in the study carrels several high school students did last-minute homework.

Julia had gone to the library out of boredom. Even after almost a year and a half, it was still hard for her to get through the weekends. Martin had worked long hours, and they barely saw each other during the week, so they had relished their time together during the weekend. She still missed him terribly every time Friday night rolled around.

She was looking through the new fiction, trying to find a good book to read. Julia loved to read, but lately it seemed that every book she started ended up depressing her. She needed something light and funny. She had rejected a dozen books already on the basis of the jacket flaps' synopsis. Too much death, too much loss, too much angst. Maybe a good mystery . . . no, too scary to read in the house alone. Even when Martin was alive, she had not read a mystery unless he was sitting in bed beside her. Silly . . .

The elevator across from the shelves where Julia stood came to a squeaking, grinding halt and the doors slid open.

Julia froze as a preoccupied Jake Brighton, his head bent reading some papers in his hand, stepped out of the elevator. Before Julia could turn away, he looked up and spotted her.

"Julia! Hello!"

She hesitated imperceptibly. "Hello."

"Sunday night at the library, huh?"

"Yeah, I guess so."

"I'm doing a little last-minute research." He waved the papers with his explanation. "We're still trying to get the school bond issue passed. I was hoping to find somewhere in all the city's archives a surefire way to convince the community to vote in favor of it." He motioned to the elevator. "There's some amazing history stored in that basement. I could have spent all evening down there. Did you know that Calypso's first school was in the old Lutheran church?"

She was having trouble being friendly, but he seemed not to notice. He went on, enthusiastically explaining his ideas for the public forum the school board had scheduled for the following week. She listened with increasing interest. Being a newcomer to the community, she was in the dark about some of the politics that had preceded this controversial election. It was rather fascinating.

Before she knew what was happening, Jake had steered her to a comfortable lounge area in the corner of the nonfiction section, and they were deep in conversation as though they were old friends.

Finally Jake said, "I'm sorry. This is probably boring you to tears. I'm just so wrapped up in this thing right now that it's all I can think about."

"No, really. It's interesting. Especially since I don't know very much about Calypso. I feel like a very well-informed voter now." She smiled. "I guess I better get down to city hall and register now, huh?"

Jake burst out laughing. "You mean I just sat here and wasted my two-hour speech on somebody who can't even vote?"

"Hey, don't you worry. By election day I'll be a bona fide Calypso registered voter."

There was an easy silence between them. Julia's reservations about Jake had vanished in his presence. Then Jake asked about Andy.

"Things are getting better. We're not home free yet, by any means, but we're making progress. His teacher told me you talked to her. I really appreciate that, Jake. You went 'above and beyond the call of duty,' if I can use an old cliché."

He waved her thanks away. "Hey, it was no big deal. Like I told you, anything that affects the kids is part of my job."

"You love kids, don't you?"

"I have ever since I started teaching. I know it sounds crazy, but I didn't decide to go into teaching because of my love for children. That came later. I was an only child, so I didn't know anything about kids. Teaching seemed to be a noble thing to do. My dad was a lawyer who chose his profession for the money it would bring, and I guess teaching was my way of rebelling against him. He ended up dying before I got my degree, so it didn't matter anyway. I have tried to redeem my wrong motives, and I think I'm in this field for the right reasons now. I really have come to love the kids."

Julia seized the opening. "Tell me about your own kids. Here you practically know Sam's and Andy's life histories, and all I know is that you have three kids. But I don't know anything about them."

"Well, Jana is married and lives in Chicago. She works for an advertising agency there, and her husband is in engineering. Brant and Kyle are both at the university in Urbana. Brant is a graduate student. He's engaged to a very sweet girl. And Kyle is doing his student teaching this semester. We're—" He stopped midsentence. "I'm . . . I'm thrilled about that, of course."

Julia could tell by his suddenly flustered manner that Jake had slipped. Julia was silent, giving him a chance to explain himself. He said nothing.

"What about their mother, Jake?"

"What?" He was floundering.

"I'm sorry," she said, waving her hand as if to dismiss her own question. "It's none of my business. I had no right to pry."

Jake sighed. "No . . . no . . ." He put his head down, obviously upset. He sighed again and haltingly told her what she already knew.

"Umm, their mother . . . umm. Julia . . . my wife has Alzheimer's disease. She doesn't live at home anymore. She's in the advanced stages, and she doesn't even know me anymore."

"Where does she live, Jake?" Julia almost felt deceitful asking a question to which she knew the answer, but she was determined to carry this conversation to its bitter end.

"She's at Parkside, Julia."

"Jake, why haven't you mentioned that before?" She

heard the hurt in her own voice and saw in his eyes that he heard it too.

"I'm not sure, Julia. I'm really not sure. I don't know if I could tell you if I did know the reason."

"What do you mean by that?"

He reached out and put his hand lightly on her arm. It was a familiar gesture. Too familiar. Julia sat motionless as Jake tried to explain.

"Julia, I'm a married man, and I love my wife, but I'm lonely. I know you can understand that. I didn't mean anything by keeping this from you. I guess . . . I guess I thought I would lose your friendship if you thought I was married."

"You mean if I *knew* you were married." She couldn't suppress her anger.

He sighed and gave her a wry smile. "Yes. If you knew I was married."

"You should have told me, Jake. I don't appreciate being toyed with."

"Hey, it wasn't like that, I promise. I enjoy your company. More than you'll ever know."

Julia brushed his hand from her arm, gathered her purse and jacket, and stood. "I have to go now."

"Julia, wait. Please, don't leave like this."

Without another word, she hurried to the front entrance and disappeared into the black night.

12

Jake saw Julia several times in the following weeks. They passed each other as she was leaving Parkside and he was arriving to visit Ellen. She pretended not to see him, ostensibly adjusting her rearview mirror as their cars met on the narrow drive. But he knew that she had recognized him. It hurt him that she wouldn't even acknowledge his presence.

Never in his life had he experienced such deep regret about something he could have changed. If only he had been honest with her from the beginning. He had blown it with his misguided attempts to keep from speaking of Ellen's existence. He knew he hadn't done it to protect Julia. If he were honest, he'd have to admit that he had been playing with fire. His motives hadn't been evil—he only wanted their friendship to go as far as propriety would allow. But that had been terribly unfair to Julia, for he hadn't considered her feelings at all. She was completely innocent in her ignorance of his marriage. If only he could be given a second chance with her. If only . . .

Jake ran into Julia again at parent-teacher conferences at the high school. This time she couldn't avoid him. But her greeting was cool and distant, and she hurried on down the hallway, obviously anxious to avoid any further conversation.

Twice Jake picked up the telephone to call her and try to explain . . . to make excuses. But he couldn't carry through with it. Everything he thought to tell her would only tangle the web further.

So he tried to put her out of his mind. The school bond had finally passed, and there was much work to be done with plans for the new school and reorganization of the other buildings in the district. He was thankful for the busyness that kept his mind off Julia. And off Ellen too.

Recently, Ellen had taken what Jake thought of as "a turn for the worse." Physically, she was much the same. But the quiet, subdued manner that first characterized Alzheimer's for Ellen had been replaced with one of agitation and frustration, manifesting itself in loud outcries. Her words were not jumbled English but alien, cacophonous babbling that Jake could hardly bear to listen to. At times she was so crazed she beat on him, her thin arms flailing impotently, as though he were to blame for the ghosts that haunted her. When her tantrums were over, she sat and wept for hours at a time. Where she got the strength for her frenzied outbursts, Jake couldn't imagine. She was thin and pale, and her eyes had a sunken, bilious look about them.

It became torture for Jake to walk through the wide doorways of Parkside each evening. No longer could he come and stay for an evening of reading and quiet companionship with Ellen. He brought his offerings of flowers, fresh laundry, or ice cream and made his escape as quickly as decorum would allow.

Jake was not the only one who found it difficult to visit

Ellen. Many of her friends from church and her fellow teachers at school had come often in the beginning. They sat quietly with Ellen, or they came in twos and threes and visited among themselves, keeping Ellen company with their conversation. But she had inflicted her tirades on them as well, and one by one they drifted away. Some sent a card now and then, but most had completely abandoned Ellen. Because of this, they avoided Jake as well.

Jake didn't fault them. He, of all people, knew how difficult it was to be with Ellen now. In reality, he didn't think Ellen understood that everyone had stopped coming to see her. But Jake knew, and it was a blow to him. He felt the rejection keenly, as though he were the rejected one.

Even Sandra could no longer stand to see Ellen the way she had become. She called Jake occasionally to ask about Ellen, but their conversation was strained, and Jake could hear the guilt in her voice. He wanted to tell her it was okay . . . that he understood. Yet he wanted her to suffer too . . . to feel shame for forsaking her best friend. Jake hated the feelings this whole miserable situation forced upon him.

Howard and MaryEllen came each week, without fail. The trip was difficult for them, and seeing Ellen deteriorate week after week only increased their pain. But Jake knew better than to ask them not to come. For them, that would have been unthinkable. Ellen's sisters came when they were in the state. Kathy lived in Indiana and came fairly often, but Diana and Carol had moved out of state and rarely got back. It was especially tough on them because they saw great leaps of decline in Ellen each time they came, and the sisters carried a measure of guilt because they couldn't be closer to help out.

One particularly difficult evening when Ellen lashed out at Jake, he fled from her room, not knowing anymore how to cope with her outbursts. He stopped off at the nurses' station and asked them to give her a sedative. Then he strode down the hall, away from Ellen's room.

What good did all his attentions do? Most of the time, she didn't even know him; when she did, she seemed to hate him. Was Ellen any better for the things he did for her? In his heart he knew she wasn't to blame for her actions. He knew she could no more control them than she could stop the Alzheimer's itself. But it was exceedingly difficult not to take it personally when the woman he had loved all his life behaved with such violence toward him.

These questions besieged him as he pushed open the front doors and breathed in the brisk air of the coming night. More and more it was sheer relief to walk out those doors.

With his head down, he started toward his car in the parking lot. It was chilly even for March, and he pulled the collar of his jacket up around his ears. In the dusky light of evening, he saw a familiar figure leaning over the hood of a car several rows down from where he was parked. He was headed toward her car to offer help before he quite realized that it was Julia. She was struggling with something on the hood of the car, and she seemed distressed.

Jake approached her, clearing his throat loudly to announce his presence and avoid startling her.

"Julia? Hi! You have car trouble?"

She was exasperated and embarrassed. "Oh, I think I locked my keys in the car. They're not in the ignition, and I've dumped my whole purse searching for them, but they're not here. I must have put them under the seat."

"Oooh, boy. Do you have a spare set anywhere?"

"At home in my desk. A lot of good they'll do me there. I kept promising myself I'd get a spare set for my billfold, but I never got around to it. With my luck, I'd lock my whole purse in the car then," she said wryly.

He laughed. "I know what you mean. In fact, I did that one time. I locked my keys in my car, and I thought I was so smart to have a spare in my wallet. Then I looked in the car and there sat my wallet on the console. Well, hey, listen . . . I'd be glad to drive you home to get the keys and bring you back here."

"Oh no. You don't need to do that. I'll figure something out."

"Seriously, Julia. I don't have a thing going on tonight. It wouldn't be any trouble at all. Besides, it's too cold to stand around here for long."

She hesitated. "Oh, Jake. I hate to put you out. Are you sure?"

"Absolutely. No problem. Come on, I'm parked over here."

She quickly stuffed everything back into her purse and followed him to his car. Jake unlocked the passenger door for her, then came around and got in behind the wheel.

"Now, let's see. Sweetbriar Lane?"

"Yes, clear east on Sweetbriar. I think it's quickest to take Third Street over to Broadway."

"Okay."

He turned onto the highway, and they rode in awkward silence for several minutes. Suddenly Julia broke the stillness, putting her hand to her mouth with a gasp.

"Oh, Jake. I can't believe I'm so stupid. My house keys are on the key ring with my car keys. I'm not going to be able to get into the house. Andy is spending the night with a friend, and Sam won't be home till after supper tonight." She put her head in her hands. "This is embarrassing. I am so sorry to cause all this trouble."

"Julia, don't worry about it. Let's see . . . do the boys have keys?"

"Yes. Sam has both house keys and car keys. He's at

Brian Baylor's house. I'd have you take me there if I knew where Brian lived. Do you know him?"

"I know who he is, but I don't have any idea where he lives. Why don't I just take you to my house, and you can call Sam from there?"

Julia was nearly squirming with embarrassment. "I should have called from Parkside. Would you mind taking me back there? I'm sorry to make you go so far out of your way."

"I don't mind at all, but I live just four blocks from here, Julia. It's a lot closer, and you'll have a comfortable place to wait."

"Okay," she said resignedly. She paused, as if trying to decide whether to say something or not, then she sighed and plunged in.

"Jake, I am really uncomfortable about this. I wouldn't blame you at all if you thought it looked like I set this whole thing up. But, honestly, I didn't."

"It never crossed my mind. Although if I'd had some time to think about it, it might have." He grinned at her, teasing, trying to put her at ease.

She didn't return his smile. She looked genuinely troubled.

He turned serious. "Hey, I believe you, Julia. I was just kidding. Honest. Listen, if anybody needs to do any explaining here, it's me." He was silent for a minute, trying to compose his thoughts. "Julia, I am sorry for the things I said in the library the other night. I had no right to say what I did. And even more than that, I was very wrong for not telling you up front about Ellen. I didn't want to say anything when we first met because I didn't want it to look like I was after your sympathy. Frankly, it was nice to relate to someone who wasn't always overcome with pity for me. Then, after we got to know each other, it seemed . . . well, I had let it go so long without telling you, I was afraid you would avoid me if you found out after all that time that I was married. I've thought about it a lot, and I know I was being very selfish and terribly unfair to you. I needed someone to talk to, and I guess in that way, I used you. I want to be careful how I say this, but . . . as attractive as you are, and as much as I enjoy talking to you, I wasn't hitting on you. I promise you that. At this point it sounds trite, but I am a pretty decent guy." He smiled in the semidarkness of the car. She did not respond, so he went on, trying to convince her.

"I love my wife, Julia, and I intend to stay faithful to her. I believe in the wedding vows . . . in sickness and in health included."

The whole time Jake was talking, Julia had sat with her head down, preoccupied with a hangnail on one of her tightly clasped fingers. Now she turned to him with a gentle smile on her face.

"Thank you, Jake. I appreciate your honesty. I'm sorry I didn't give you a chance to explain that night at the library. I shouldn't have run out on you like that. I was angry . . . and to be honest, I was disappointed in you. It bothered me a great deal that you led me to believe you were unmarried, and then out of the blue to find out not only do you have a wife, but she lives at Parkside. It just seemed like the subject might have come up once or twice." She gave him a chastening smile.

"You're right. I plead guilty." They were pulling in to Jake's driveway. "Julia, I don't know if you will believe this, but I'm not usually a liar. I know I was deceitful about Ellen. I realize now how terribly wrong that was, and I'm truly sorry. I've asked the Lord's forgiveness, and if you can forgive me, I'd like to start over." He got out of the car and went around to open her door.

His voice took on a goofy, prim and proper tenor. He

bowed as he opened her door. "Good evening, ma'am. I'm Jake Brighton. I live right here at 245 Oaklawn. My wife, Ellen, lives at Parkside, and we have three beautiful children together." He knew it sounded corny, but he wanted to make her laugh, to lighten the moment.

She grinned up at him, got out of the car, and followed him up the walk to the front door. He unlocked the door and stepped back to let her in first. She admired the old house, and he led her through the main rooms on the first floor. They chatted cordially while Jake gave her a tour. While she admired, he bragged on Ellen's taste in decorating the house. It felt good to be open with Julia about Ellen and not have to carefully weigh his words.

"Would you like something to drink? Iced tea?"

"That'd be great. Don't go to any trouble though."

"No trouble. I made sun tea this morning. Do you take sugar?"

"Mmm. Sounds great. No, no sugar."

While Julia tried to reach Sam, Jake poured tea over ice in tall glasses and brought them into the living room.

Julia hung up the phone and reported that the boys were playing basketball, but Mrs. Baylor wasn't sure where. They probably wouldn't be back for another hour. Julia had explained the situation to her and arranged to call back later. Jake suggested that they grab a bite to eat while they waited. Reluctantly, Julia accepted the invitation.

They went to a small cafe near Jake's house and ordered burgers and fries. Their conversation came easier now that they had cleared the air. Wanting to begin anew in complete honesty with Julia, Jake told her about the rough day he'd had with Ellen. He poured out the whole story from the beginning, and concluded, "It's devastating to have her vent her rage on me. I honestly don't think she has any idea who

I am, but still, it's hard not to take it personally. I feel so frustrated for her."

"Oh, Jake, I just can't imagine how awful it must be to have someone die before your eyes like that. You know, I was so angry because I didn't get to tell Martin goodbye, but this must be much worse. You have to say goodbye every day."

Julia's face had softened, and Jake could hear in her voice that her sympathy was genuine. "That says it perfectly. I feel like Ellen has died over and over. In many ways it would have been easier if she had just suddenly died one day. This has been . . . I don't know . . . a walking death, I guess. Ellen has been dying a day at a time. We've lost one thing after another, and I know it will continue that way, until finally, there's nothing left at all. This is a terrible disease, Julia . . . it's simply terrible." He stared into his coffee mug, afraid of breaking down in front of her.

When he looked up, he saw there were tears in Julia's eyes. He went on, emboldened by her sincere attentiveness, her sensitivity. "First I lost my confidante. Communication was always an essential part of our relationship. Ellen and I talked all the time—about everything. There was nothing we couldn't tell each other. It seems so cruel that one of the first things the Alzheimer's took from her was her ability to speak—or at least to speak sensibly." Jake shrugged and shook his head, feeling anew his perplexity at the way things had turned out.

"After that, things continued to get worse. I lost my helpmate. Ellen was a teacher, and we frequently worked together on projects at school—things that involved the students. Only a year after she was diagnosed with Alzheimer's, she had to quit teaching. About the same time, I started doing all the cooking and shopping. We finally hired someone to clean when she couldn't handle that anymore. Of course, eventually, we needed someone at the house all the time."

The waitress brought their food and they picked at it in silence for a few minutes. Neither of them was hungry, except for conversation. He told her then about the awful day that Ellen had run away, and about the excruciating decision he'd had to make to put her in Parkside.

Jake struggled with how much he should say. Julia was so understanding that it was tempting to tell her more than maybe he should, but he went on. "Then I lost my lover. When Ellen didn't know me anymore—or worse, when she thought I was her father or one of the boys—it just didn't seem right to . . . well, you know what I mean." He paused, overcome with emotion. Though he willed them away, tears filled his eyes. "When Ellen first moved to Parkside, at least she was still a companion to me. I could go and just sit with her. I felt it meant something to her . . . that I was helping her by being there. And it eased my loneliness too. But now, I don't even have that. I don't have any part of Ellen anymore, Julia."

"You still have the memories, Jake," she said quietly.

"I do. But I have to work so hard to conjure them up, it sometimes doesn't seem worth it. The truth is, Ellen is a totally different person now. I feel as though my Ellen has been dead for years. Alzheimer's is cruel . . . it has totally robbed her of her personality. There is nothing left of the old Ellen." Jake's eyes were unfocused, staring into the face of the past. He began to remember now, and the remembering was made easier because Julia was there to share it.

"Ellen was funny and smart and strong. She loved to argue"—he chuckled as he suddenly saw Ellen's furrowed brow, and the expression she always wore during a good row—"but she never held a grudge. And she was such a good mother. We lost a baby at birth—our first—and I think Ellen treasured the other three that much more because of it. It makes me angry that she'll never be able to see what our kids have become. We had so many big plans for these years. We wanted to travel. Ellen always wanted to go to Europe. . . ." His voice trailed off again, remembering. "Yet, I'm grateful this happened after the kids were grown and away from home. It would have been far worse to deal with it while they were still home. But, oh, I'd give anything if Ellen could see how happy Jana is . . . how much Brant likes his job . . . how excited Kyle is about student teaching. I think you probably understand more than anyone how the joy diminishes when you can no longer share these things with the one you love—the one with whom you gave life to your children."

"I do understand that, Jake. I would never tell my children this, but when Martin died, it was as though their lives became a little less, somehow. It's hard to explain, but their father was so much a part of them, and even though I see him in both of the boys, it's not the same now that he is gone. It's like he was the standard for comparison, and now there is no standard. Does that make sense?"

"I think so."

"Martin was such a strong person. He wasn't perfect, and I've tried to be careful not to put him on a pedestal like widows often do. But he had a . . . a presence about him—a strength. The boys don't have it . . . at least not yet. I think sometimes I fault them for that. Maybe it would have been easier if we'd had girls. Maybe I wouldn't have expected so much from Martin's daughters."

"And maybe you would have expected more. One thing I've learned, Julia, is that it doesn't pay to play the 'if only' game. It's hard enough to get through what is, without worrying about what might have been."

"I know you're right. But that's something I've always found difficult. I'm too analytical, I guess. And I do play the 'if only' game. Oh, I lay awake those first nights torturing myself. If only I'd insisted we get new tires on the car. If only I hadn't told him that morning to hurry home . . ." She paused and Jake didn't fill the silence.

"I was so lonely—so terribly lonely. You know, when Martin went away on a business trip—even a long one—I often thought, 'this isn't so bad . . . I could make it as a widow.' But I had no idea . . . *no idea* of the loneliness—the emptiness you feel when someone you love is gone forever from your life."

Suddenly, as though a revelation struck her, she looked at Jake. "That's how it is with Ellen, isn't it? She's . . . she's gone forever from your life."

He just nodded.

They had barely touched their food, taking sustenance in the conversation instead. The waitress cleared their dishes away, Jake paid the check, and they got into the car. It was dark, and as they drove back to his house, talking, Jake watched Julia's expressions in the ebb and flow of the yellow light cast by the streetlamps they passed. With fascination, he saw her hands echo the words she spoke.

They went inside and Julia called the Baylors again. She relayed to Jake that Sam was back, and she had arranged to meet him at the house. When they pulled into Julia's driveway, Sam wasn't there yet, so they sat in the car and continued their conversation.

Julia began to tell Jake about the dreadful day that Martin had been killed. Her voice was detached, as though she were telling someone else's story. Jake could see by the faraway look in her eyes that Julia was reliving the day as she spoke—of going to school to get the boys . . . of the horror of telling her sons that their father was dead.

"That was the most difficult thing I have ever done in my life, Jake. I went to Andy's class first . . . I'm not sure why . . . isn't that strange? I don't remember why I went there first." Her voice rose with emotion and questioning, and she looked up at Jake.

Then a glazed look crept into her eyes again. "I remember Andy came bounding out of the classroom with a huge smile on his face—like I'd come to bring him a wonderful surprise or something. I . . . I don't remember what I said, but I didn't want to give him the news inside the school, so I made him come outside with me. Then he was sure I had a surprise for him. I must have been calm because he . . . he was babbling on—trying to guess the surprise. He thought we had a new car. He guessed that we were going to visit his grandparents. He guessed a pony! A pony! I . . . I couldn't . . . I couldn't make myself tell him to stop the guessing. And then . . . then I had to tell him his daddy was gone . . . forever. I've never felt like such a traitor. I will never forget the . . . the look in his eyes . . ." Suddenly, her voice broke. She put her fist to her mouth to hold back the sobs. But they came anyway. She wept bitterly, unable to speak.

Jake was overcome with emotion. He felt the well of tears behind his eyelids, hot and threatening to spill. He leaned across the seat and took Julia in his arms. Tenderly at first, then with passion. Almost instinctively he took her face in his hands, felt the smoothness of her damp skin against his palms. Before she could struggle free, he realized what was happening and backed away in horror at his own unbridled desire.

"Oh, Julia. I am so sorry. Please . . . I didn't mean for that to happen. I had no right . . ."

But she was already out of the car . . . running for the front porch. He got out of the car and ran after her. Halfway up the steps he grabbed her shoulders and turned her toward him.

He looked straight into her eyes and spoke firmly. "Julia, I was wrong. I promise you that will never happen again."

She was shaking. "It wasn't just you, Jake. I'm guilty too. And you're right; it won't happen again."

They heard a car approaching, and Jake dropped his hands from her shoulders. The car slowed and turned into the driveway behind Jake's car. Sam got out and waved as the Baylors backed out of the drive. Then he ran up onto the porch.

"Hi, Sam," Julia said with feigned cheeriness. "This is Jake Brighton. He's the superintendent of schools, remember? Jake, this is Sam."

Jake extended his hand, and Sam shook it, a questioning look on his face.

"I rescued your mom in the parking lot at Parkside. Seems she locked every key she owns in the car."

"Yeah, that's what Brian's mom said. Well, thanks a lot for bringing her home. I've got my keys." He waved them in the air as proof.

Jake turned to Julia. "Can I give you a ride back to your car?"

"No . . . thanks. You've done more than enough." She winced at the double meaning of her words. "I do appreciate everything, Jake. Thank you. We'll be fine now."

"Okay," he said reluctantly. "Well, I'll be seeing you. . . ."

Julia watched Jake pull out of the driveway while Sam unlocked the front door. She made excuses to Sam and hurried into the bathroom, locking the door behind her. She turned on the sink faucet full force to drown out her cries. Then she sat on the side of the bathtub and sobbed.

13

Jake drove home from Julia's house in a daze. He tried to make sense of all that had happened that night but found himself more confused than ever.

One thing he knew for certain: he did not want to have to dread running into Julia the way he had after their confrontation in the library.

When he felt sure that Sam would be asleep, he dialed her number. She answered on the second ring.

"Julia. Hi. It's Jake."

"Hi."

"I just wanted to make sure everything is okay between us. Are you all right?"

"I think so. I'm . . . I'm still trying to sort things out."

"Me too. But I don't want you to worry that what happened tonight will ever happen again. Okay?"

"I trust you. We got caught up in the emotions of the moment, that's all. And I was as much to blame as you, Jake. I'm sorry. Please don't feel guilty."

"Well, it's a little late for that. I do feel very guilty. But it's over now . . . let's go on from here."

"Okay."

"Did you get your car?"

"No. A woman I work with is going to pick me up to-morrow, and I'll get it after work."

"Oh. Good."

Silence.

"Julia, would you have dinner with me tomorrow night?"

"Jake, I don't think that would be a good idea. That's too much like a date, I'm afraid."

"Well . . . how about going jogging with me? Would you feel comfortable with that?"

There was such a long silence that Jake wondered if they'd been cut off. He gave her an excuse. "We're both go-ing to be running anyway."

He heard her sigh on the other end of the line. "Julia?"

"Okay. I'll meet you at the park. What time?"

"Would seven-thirty be all right?"

"Okay. We should be done with supper by then. I'll see you then."

"Okay. Good-night."

"Good-night, Jake."

—◦◦◦—

Running in the park became their habit. There they felt safe from their own emotions, and it didn't seem improper for them to be seen together in a public place. As wonderful as it was, Calypso was still a small town. Jake was well aware that gossip spread faster than wildfire here, and the last thing he wanted was rumor of a scandal. They were careful to come and go alone, and to keep their distance physically.

For a while Jake was elated with the headiness of their

blossoming friendship. There were moments, though, when guilt bore down on him . . . when he realized that his visits to Ellen were becoming more brief. He knew he must force himself to stay longer each evening and to endure Ellen's angry outbursts more stoically than before.

He rationalized, perhaps justifiably so, that Julia's friendship fortified him for the agony he faced with Ellen. The promise of Julia's support and encouragement did help him bear the visits each evening. Knowing that in a few minutes he could pour out his anguish to Julia, he found himself being more gentle and compassionate with Ellen.

He had never been in better physical shape in his life. They were running three or four miles several times a week, and only the foulest weather kept them from meeting at the park those evenings at seven-thirty. Often their cooldown time stretched into an hour of walking and talking.

Occasionally Julia expressed concern that she was spending too much time away from the boys, but still she was there each evening, waiting for Jake.

One night, though, she told Jake—rather evasively, he thought—that she wouldn't be there the next evening, a Friday night.

"Oh? Why, you have a date?" Jake teased in the intimate repartee they had established.

But she was serious. "Yes, Jake. I do."

He literally stopped in his tracks. He stood there, breathing hard, with his hands on his waist. "Are you serious?"

"Yes, I am." She kept running, and he had to hurry to catch up with her.

"May I ask with whom?"

"His name is Bill Morland. He works at Parkside."

"Oh." Jake didn't know what else to say. He knew Bill Morland. He was the assistant administrator of Parkside.

He was good-looking, divorced, and quite honestly, Jake couldn't stand the man.

They jogged along in silence for almost a mile. Finally Julia asked almost rhetorically, for she knew the answer, "Why so quiet?"

"No reason."

She started in like a house afire. "Jake, you and I are just friends, remember? I would like to get married again someday. I'm finding that a little difficult to work toward when I haven't had one date since Martin died." Her tone was angry and sarcastic now.

"Well, you could do a lot better than Bill Morland." His anger matched her own.

"Oh, for heaven's sake! Who did you have in mind, Your Majesty?"

Jake threw his hands up. "Hey, it's none of my business. You go out with whomever you want." He pulled ahead of her then and sprinted back to his car, leaving her gaping after him.

He reached in through the open window of his car and pulled out a towel. He stood there wiping the sweat from his face and neck and then threw the towel to the floor of the car in anger. He got in and screeched out of the parking lot. He knew he was acting like an immature, impetuous teenager, but he felt powerless to stop himself.

At home he got into the shower and let the force of the hot water soothe his anger. He was being ridiculous. He had no claim on Julia whatsoever. His little tantrum in the park had betrayed his true feelings for her, both to himself and to Julia. He owed her an apology.

He tried to call her all evening, but there was no answer. At eleven o'clock he finally gave up and went to bed. He lay awake for a long time wrestling with his conscience. He knew only two things. He didn't want to lose Julia. But he couldn't have her.

———◦◦◦———

Two weeks passed and Julia didn't show up at the park. Jake went every evening, hoping against hope she would be there, and deeply disappointed when she wasn't.

One Friday night three weeks after their fight, he got out of his car, broke into a run, and she materialized at his side. He tried not to give away the wild pounding of his heart.

"Well, look who's here," he said as casually as he could manage.

"Hi."

"Julia, I'm sorry . . ."

"Hey. Forget it. I shouldn't have gotten so mad. Let's just forget it and pick up where we left off."

"Umm . . . where we left off . . . I believe you called me 'Your Majesty,' and I peeled out of the parking lot like a spoiled brat."

She laughed. "Well, then let's start from the day before that."

"Deal."

They shook on it, and he had to struggle to resist the temptation to pull her into a grateful embrace. His relief at their reconciliation was boundless. A nagging knowledge that they would eventually have to deal with this again ate at him; but he pushed it away and took each day as it came, trying not to look too far into the future.

———◦◦◦———

Christmas went by more easily than it had in four years. For the first time since Ellen had moved to Parkside, Jake didn't bring her home for the holiday. She had become calmer in the past few months, partly due to a new medication that her doctor had prescribed. But any change in her routine seemed to cause her anxiety; therefore, the doctor recommended they bring Christmas to her rather than taking her home. It was a nice Christmas, both at Parkside and back at the house on Oaklawn. The kids were all home, and Ellen's parents were there, of course. They had visited Ellen in the afternoon, taking the gifts there to be opened, but the real celebration had taken place at the house. It was almost as though they were weaning themselves from Ellen. Her absence wasn't felt quite so keenly now that everyone was accustomed to her being at Parkside and Jake being alone in the big house.

With Christmas over, the day of Brant and Cynthia's wedding was fast approaching. Jake was grateful for all the preparation involved in getting this son of his married. It took his mind off the worries about Ellen—and off the guilt about Julia.

He had no idea that the groom's parents had so many responsibilities. There were tuxedos to order, a rehearsal dinner to plan, gifts to buy. It was a bittersweet time for Jake. He remembered so clearly the joy he and Ellen had felt when they planned Jana's wedding. He longed for the old Ellen terribly—both for sharing the happiness of this occasion and for the practical help she would have been. He knew nothing about wedding etiquette, though Jana was very helpful when she could find the time. If he asked for it, Julia gave him advice, too, but her help had to be from afar.

Jake and Julia had agreed it would be best not to mention their friendship to the children. Julia's boys, because their allegiance to their father was still so fresh, might not understand Jake's place in Julia's life. Jake's kids lived far enough away that there was no need to explain it to them and risk a misunderstanding. Jake felt somewhat troubled that they had this secret to keep. It seemed to degrade their friendship. But they had talked about it at length and both felt it was best this way. So they continued week after week, meeting in the park, playing therapist to each other, and growing closer day by day.

⁂

One evening as they jogged in the park, they came face-to-face with Sandra Brenner. Jake was clearly embarrassed. Stuttering and stammering, he introduced her to Julia, deftly skirting any mention of relationships. Sandra shook Julia's hand warmly, and giving Jake a knowing smile, she jogged on.

That night when Jake was getting ready for bed, the phone rang.

"Jake, hi. This is Sandra."

He steeled himself. "Hi, Sandra."

"Jake, I just want to put your mind at ease. I know you were uncomfortable introducing me to your girlfriend. I just want you to know that I understand. And I'm happy for you. If anyone deserves to have some happiness, it's you."

"Sandra, you misunderstood." Jake was angry. "Julia is a good friend, nothing more."

"Somehow, I find that hard to believe, Jake."

"Well, don't go jumping to conclusions. That's not fair, Sandra."

"Well, Jake, I'll take your word for it. But I think Ellen would understand if—what's her name, Julia?—were more than a friend. I don't think Ellen or anyone else would judge you if you found someone else. Ellen is the same as dead, Jake. I admire your devotion to her, but don't be too hard on yourself."

"Ellen is very much alive, Sandra Brenner. If you'd go visit her once in a while you might know that."

"I'm sorry, Jake." She sounded truly repentant. "I shouldn't have said that. But you know what I mean. She's not going to get any better, and, Jake, it's not as though you're going to hurt her. She won't know. I've visited her recently enough to know that."

"Well, thank you for your opinion—I think. But please don't start any rumors, Sandra. I assure you, Julia and I are friends—nothing more."

Angry and worried, Jake hung up the phone. It sounded so cheap to hear Julia called his "girlfriend." He wasn't sure if he could trust Sandra. He had told her the truth, and he would feel awful if rumors started going around town to the contrary.

But Sandra had planted a seed in his mind. Would anyone judge him? Could he be justified if this friendship were more? He brushed the thoughts aside, but the seed germinated somewhere in the back of his mind.

※

Jake began to worry about Julia. She had been depressed since Christmas and had begun to drop hints to Jake intimating she wanted to break off their friendship. He knew that she longed to be married again. She had dated off and on, but hadn't met anyone yet that she wanted to date steadily. She usually told Jake when she had a date, partly because she had to break their jogging trysts. He was miserable when he knew she was out with another man. *Another man* . . . as though *he* was her man. Jake pushed the thought out of his mind. He had begun to do that a lot lately—because he was married, and they were just friends—push out all thoughts that crowded in about them being more than friends.

The morning of the wedding, a gray fog hung over Chicago and the January air was frigid, but Brant's spirits were buoyant. Jake, Brant, and Kyle drove to Chicago early in the day and dropped their garment bags and shaving kits off at Mark and Jana's apartment. Then Mark took them to a basketball court at the community gym where they played a cutthroat game of two-on-two. They came back to the apartment in high spirits and took turns showering, shaving, and eating the sandwiches Jana had waiting for them. She clucked over them like a mother hen, straightening their ties and spit-licking Kyle's hair till he threatened to do her bodily harm. It heartened Jake to see his kids enjoying one another and looking forward to a happy occasion together. There had been too many somber meetings between them lately. And while Ellen's absence was keenly felt, they had each come to terms with it in their own way.

Jana, especially, seemed to have a new peace about her mother. She drove to Calypso several times each month to visit Ellen at Parkside. She stopped by the house afterward, usually declaring to Jake how good all the staff were to Ellen and how nice her room was, as if convincing herself that sending Ellen to Parkside had been the right thing to do after all.

Marriage agreed with Jana. She looked radiant in the cranberry-colored satin dress she had bought for the wedding. Her hair was cut in a new, shorter style, and Jake was startled by how much she looked like Ellen.

Finally it was time to leave for the church. The ceremony began at four o'clock, and though the fog had not lifted, inside the chapel was beautiful in candlelight and simple ivy greenery.

Brant and Cynthia had chosen to have a small wedding.

Only Kyle and Cynthia's sister stood with them as attendants. Their closest friends and family waited expectantly, scattered throughout the first few pews.

Jake felt a surge of happiness for Brant as he met his bride at the altar. Cynthia was breathtakingly beautiful in the elegant white gown. Her blue eyes met Brant's, and the love they shared was unmistakable.

Jake's throat swelled with emotion—joy and pride in this handsome, noble son who stood before him, and great hope for the future that Brant and Cynthia had ahead of them. Yet underneath the joyous sentiments lay a deep sorrow for what they all had lost. The contrast between Brant and Cynthia's closeness and Jake's utter loneliness was acutely painful.

Two voices began to quarrel inside his mind. He felt as though he stood on the brink of a crucial decision—perhaps a life-changing decision. Surely he deserved the love and companionship that Julia had added to his life. The thought of her brought a smile to his lips.

He knew he could not go on with Julia as they had been. The passion was too great. There was much more between them than friendship, and it begged to be fulfilled. He had grieved—oh, how he had grieved for Ellen. But she was gone. She was virtually dead. There was so little left of Ellen's spirit—the Ellen that he had loved. It was hard for Jake to visit her anymore. He was faithful to go to her nearly every day, but it had been months since she had uttered his name. And though the tantrums had abated, the constant nonsensical jabbering repulsed him. It hurt to be repulsed by someone who had once been so dear to him. *Once* was the operative word. There was nothing left of Ellen that was dear to him now . . . nothing but memories. It was Julia who was dear to him. She was alive and vibrant and responsive. He loved her! He hadn't really admitted it to himself until now. He knew she loved him, too, even though they had not yet spoken the words. He was certain she loved him. And he needed so to be loved right now.

The organ stopped playing, and an expectant hush fell over the small sanctuary. The minister, his hair and beard white with age, but his voice rich and sonorous, began the litany of the marriage ceremony. Cynthia's father gave his daughter's hand to Brant, and the couple turned to face each other. Brant repeated the vows after the minister. "I, Brant, take thee, Cynthia, to be my lawful wedded wife. To have and to hold from this day forward . . ."

Brant's next words gripped Jake like a vise, and the argument in his mind became fierce. ". . . for better or for worse . . ." He and Ellen had shared so many years of "for better"—now he was living "for worse."

". . . for richer, for poorer, in sickness and in health . . ." But this was a sickness that had no end, yet it was like a death. Ellen would never recover. Sandra was right. Ellen may as well be dead.

". . . to love and to cherish from this day forward . . ." He had loved and cherished Ellen—with all of his heart. He had been good to her. He had taken care of her—was still taking care of her. And he would continue to do so. Julia would help him take care of her. They would never let their love abandon Ellen.

Then Brant spoke the words that would forever transform Jake. "And to thee only will I cleave, as long as we both shall live."

"Thee only . . . thee only . . . thee only"—the words echoed over and over in Jake's mind—*"as long as we both shall live."* Jake felt physically sick and a wave of nausea washed over him. He felt sick at heart, too, his conscience pierced to the quick. The truth that had been veiled to him lay stark and naked in front of him. He could not avoid it. Jake Brigh-

ton had once stood before a holy altar and spoken a solemn promise to *his* bride. Many years and much sorrow lay in between, but, nevertheless, it was an eternal promise he had made. Even before that, before he had ever met Ellen—the picture of that young college boy standing in a lonely dorm room, his father's crumpled obituary in hand, was vividly clear in Jake's mind. He had taken an oath to be the husband that his father had never been.

A crystal recollection of that resolve came back to him now. Jake Brighton was a man of his word. Could he face his children, could he face Howard and MaryEllen, or the memory of Oscar and Hattie; indeed, could he face himself, if he carried out what he had sat in this church—this hallowed place—and planned to do? He knew now that the precipice he had meant to plummet from was his very *honor*. He had tried to justify his love for Julia, because, in a way, it *was* a pure love. There had been only one embrace, and they had both fled from that. Yet, the truth was that every time he saw Julia, every time he heard her husky voice, he was stirring embers of passion that threatened to burst into flame.

Like all bridegrooms, he had made his promise to Ellen without knowing what the future held. Now it was time to redeem that promise.

Could he bear to give up Julia? She had been the only light in the nightmare he was living. Though he loved her with all his heart, he knew for certain he could not continue to see her without tarnishing his honor, without defiling the holy ground of his marriage.

He stood at a crossroads, on the verge of trespass. He felt deep sadness, but stronger than the sadness was the peace that poured over him when he resolved to do the thing he knew he must now do.

Oh, God. I've been so blind, he prayed silently. *Please for-*

give me, please! And give me the strength I need....

Cynthia was speaking her vows now. In the quiet of his heart, Jake echoed the words, renewing the promises he had made to Ellen at that altar so long ago. *I, Jake, take thee, Ellen . . . in sickness and in health, to love and to cherish from this day forward, and* to thee only will I cleave as long as we both shall live . . . *as long as it takes, El.*

What happened next, Jake could only call a miracle. Outside the chapel windows, the fog lifted almost instantaneously, and rays of sunlight flooded through the stained-glass windows. The sanctuary was bathed in a golden light that was almost tangible. He would have thought it an apparition that only he had seen had he not heard the audible gasp of the congregation. Jake felt that he had received a holy blessing. What had begun as a willful decision to love Ellen anew, in an instant became a full-fledged emotion. A new, pure love for his wife washed over him like a fountain, and he felt the cleansing the fountain offered as surely as though it were streams of water.

14

In spite of Jake's sadness at knowing he must say goodbye to Julia, peace engulfed him, wrapping him in a blanket of assurance. He was doing the right thing.

It would be right for Julia too. It had been unfair to tie her to himself as he had. Genuine love would let her go . . . would free her to find someone to share her life completely, as he was unable to do.

He had been flirting dangerously with sin, and he was ashamed as the revelation unfolded. He had tried to fool himself into believing that he was above temptation, but now he saw how close he had come to falling. He saw that he had held God at arm's length, fearful of coming into the Light, lest the true motives and intentions of his heart be revealed.

His deepest guilt was that he had carried Julia along in the charade. Now he had to tell her his transgression, and he knew it would hurt her deeply.

He surprised himself by not worrying about what he

would say to her. He knew the words would be there when the time came.

⁂

They sent Brant and Cynthia off on their honeymoon in a shower of good wishes and love. Jake and Kyle stayed with Mark and Jana Saturday night. Early Sunday afternoon Kyle caught a ride back to school with a friend who lived in Chicago. Jake left a few hours later.

The ride back to Calypso was lonely compared to the revelry of the drive into Chicago with the boys. But he was glad for the time alone to think and to pray about the changes he needed to make in his life . . . and about how he would tell Julia.

He wanted to make a clean break. He didn't want to leave her hanging in any way. He had cheated her long enough of the chance to start a new life and make new friends and meet someone who could share her life.

In many ways she was still grieving Martin, even though it had been over two years since Martin's accident. It was partly Jake's fault that she still grieved, for he had put her in a limbo that had forbidden her to move forward in the process of letting Martin go. Jake knew Julia wouldn't see it that way, but he saw many things clearly now. His decision had illuminated many truths that he had been completely blind to before.

In spite of the gnawing sadness, in spite of the aching emptiness he already felt at the thought of losing Julia, he felt like a new man . . . a man reborn. It amazed him. It was liberating to be doing the right thing, and to know without a doubt that it was right.

Jake turned onto Oaklawn just as the sun was sinking below the rooftops. The old house hadn't looked so warm and friendly in a long time. Even the stark gray branches of the January trees looked welcoming, ushering him home.

He wanted to call Julia . . . to warn her. It didn't seem right to spring this on her without preparing her. He wanted her to have time to see, as he did, that his decision was right.

He showered and dressed, then went to the phone on his nightstand and dialed her number. Suddenly, as the phone rang on the other end, and he realized he was about to hear her voice, his resolve began to weaken for the first time since Brant's wedding. He steeled himself to go through with it.

"Hello?"

"Julia, it's Jake."

"Jake! Hi!" He didn't often call her at home. She sounded surprised. "How did the wedding go?"

"It was beautiful. It was a nice weekend." Unexpectedly, sadness overwhelmed him. This was goodbye, and he knew she heard it in his voice.

"Jake? Is everything all right?"

"Oh, Julia. It is, and it isn't."

"What's wrong?" There was deep concern in her voice.

"I have to talk to you, Julia. But not on the phone." Impulsively he asked her, "Could you get away tonight for a while?"

"The boys are at Martin's folks. They won't be back till around ten. Do you want to come over here?"

He hesitated. He had never been in her house before. "Yes, if you're okay with that. Ten minutes?"

"Yes, that'll be fine."

He felt as though he'd already blown it. He had her worried sick. He could hear the questioning in her voice. Well, at least she wouldn't have to suffer long. In an hour it would all be over. *They* would be over.

He drove through the streets of Calypso, quiet on a Sunday evening in winter. Julia's porch light was on. Jake parked on the street and walked across the front lawn. She met him at the door and let him in without a word.

Her house looked much as he had imagined it. Earthy colors. Just cluttered enough to be warm and welcoming. One wall across from the fireplace lined with bookshelves, original paintings on the wall, classical music on the stereo.

She led him to the sofa in front of the fireplace where a huge log crackled and spat at the grate. She sat down across from him in Martin's recliner, pulling her stockinged feet up under her.

"Tell me."

Her words shocked Jake. They reverberated back through the years. They were the same two words Ellen had spoken that night forever ago when they had found out about the Alzheimer's. How many times would he have to answer these words of a woman he loved?

"Julia, something happened to me at Brant's wedding. I'm not sure I can explain it clearly to you, but it's . . . it's as if I've been blind for a long time, and suddenly, now I can see. Oh . . . where do I start?" He sighed and fell quiet, thinking. He was glad that Julia didn't try to fill the silence.

Finally he said, "Julia, I'm going to tell you some things tonight that I've never told you. But before I say anything else, I must tell you that I came here tonight to say goodbye. When I leave here, it will be for the last time. I don't want there to be any misunderstanding about that."

Julia's bottom lip began to tremble, and tears began to fall, unblotted, down her cheeks. Jake saw her reaction to his words, and it tugged at his heart, but he knew he had to continue.

"Julia, I have been fooling myself . . . I think we've both been fooling ourselves. We thought we could be just friends, but for me, at least, that's been impossible. I'm pretty sure it's been impossible for you too.

"As much as I didn't intend to, I've fallen in love with you." He held up his hand. "It may not be appropriate for me to tell you this now, but I want you to know that you're a woman a man can easily fall in love with. Julia, I know you'll find someone and get married again. I've tied you down in the name of friendship, and that hasn't been fair to you. There's been a lot of unfairness all around on my part." Jake hung his head, struck anew with shame over what he had almost allowed to happen.

"More than anyone, I haven't been fair to Ellen. At Brant's wedding, when he and Cynthia started saying their vows, I felt as though a bolt of lightning went straight through me. Julia, I stood at an altar nearly thirty years ago and promised Ellen that I would love her in sickness and in health. And I have . . . I've never stopped loving her . . . the real Ellen. But there's another phrase in the vows that says 'and to thee only will I cleave.' I made that promise to Ellen also. I promised it for as long as we both should live. If I stay with you another day, Julia, I will break every one of those vows. I cannot do that."

He told her then about his father and about the oath he had taken when his father died. He realized now that the reason he had never told her the story before was that it would have required too much of him. He would have had to face the duplicity of his behavior and the compromise of his principles. He hadn't been willing for that.

"Julia, I know I will never have Ellen back the way she was, but I renewed those vows to her this weekend, and God has renewed my love for her. I can't explain it, and I know it won't be easy, but I intend to keep every one of my marriage vows if it kills me.

"Oh, Julia, if we had met in another time, another place . . ." His voice trailed off. Hadn't he always told her it was no use thinking about what might have been?

213

"Julia, you've been a great joy to me, but in these past weeks you've also become a great temptation, and I don't think those two things can be allowed to exist in the same person. Most importantly, I've kept you from going on with your life. For that, I need to ask your forgiveness. I recognize that I've been flirting with sin, and I'm so sorry that I involved you. Please forgive me, Julia. I've been so wrong."

He went on to tell her all the thoughts he had pondered since Brant's wedding—how he had prevented her from grieving for Martin as she should, how unfair he had been to tie her to himself. And when all his words were finished, he waited for her to speak.

She got up and went for a box of tissues. When she sat down again, she blew her nose and wiped away the mascara that smudged her cheeks. She looked beautiful in the light of the dying embers. On the stereo, a violin concerto played softly, making the moment unbearably heartrending. Jake almost asked her to turn the stereo off, but somehow the music seemed fitting, and he let it go. She looked at him and spoke in her soft, throaty voice.

"Jake, it's probably no surprise when I say that I've fallen in love with you, also. And I love you all the more for what you've just told me. You see, I love you because of your trustworthiness, your integrity, your sense of honor. I've been in such a turmoil since I first realized that I love you. I knew if I could get you to declare your love for me, then you weren't the man I thought you were. If you were that man of integrity, then I knew I could never have you." She smiled sadly. "Now I have the best of both worlds: I know that you love me, and you still have your honor. I do forgive you, Jake. In the deepest part of my heart, I haven't felt right about us. I need your forgiveness too . . . for not listening to God's gentle voice warning me. I was an accomplice, Jake, and I'm sorry." Again, her smile was sad. "Thank you,

Jake. Though it doesn't feel like it now, I know this decision is a gift. I know it is right. And I know God will bless it."

They sat together and shared aloud how blind they each had been to think their friendship was right when they had felt the need to keep it secret. She had neglected her boys at a time when they needed her desperately; he had given his time and energy to her, rather than to Ellen. Further, their growing love for each other had forced them to turn from God for fear of their relationship being exposed for what it really was.

In a new love of unblemished purity, they released each other forever. Jake rose to go, and Julia followed him to the door. He did not embrace her or even touch her. Jake didn't trust himself yet, and he knew Julia understood his weakness.

He turned out of her driveway, not toward Oaklawn, but toward his true home—where Ellen was.

⁂

It was after nine when he walked through the front doors of Parkside. The nurses' aides were in Ellen's room, helping her get ready for bed.

"Thank you." He dismissed them politely.

Ellen stood statuelike in the middle of the room with her back toward Jake. He went to her, and putting his hands gently on her shoulders, he turned her to face him, saying her name softly. Her eyes showed no recognition, but she gave him a wan smile. She wore a long flannel nightgown, and behind the vacant eyes, she was still beautiful. He led her to the chair by her window. He picked up her hairbrush from the bureau and began to brush her hair with gentle strokes, surprised at the familiar feel of the soft curls. It had been so long since he had touched her in such an intimate way. She was quiet, alone in that faraway place of hers. Jake smoothed her hair with his hands, moved by the tenderness his actions evoked. He poured her a glass of water and held the cup while she drank from it. Then he turned the bed down and helped her swing her legs over the side. He plumped her pillow and gently tucked the blankets around her. She closed her eyes peacefully. He pulled a chair beside her bed and watched her sleep, memories of their shared past floating in the semidarkness until the lights in the hallway were dimmed.

Then he went home and climbed into his own bed, at peace with himself and at peace with God.

He knew it wouldn't always be this easy. He knew there might be babbling and tantrums, and uncontrollable weeping in their future together. He also knew that he had done the right thing. He could look in the mirror and, without shame, face the man he saw reflected there. Whatever he must bear in the days to come, he knew his faith and God's grace would bring him across to the other side, however wide the chasm might be.

His Bible was lying on the nightstand, and he noticed with chagrin that a fine layer of dust had gathered on its dark cover. He opened the book and leafed through the pages, yearning for comfort and confirmation. Under his fingers the pages fell open to the book of Job, and the words jumped off the page as though they were printed in boldface: "Though He slay me, yet will I hope in Him. . . . Indeed, this will turn out for my deliverance. . . ."

Jake closed the book and fell to his knees in gratitude.

15

The pungent scent of woodsmoke hung in the crisp autumn air, and the yellow leaves clung tenaciously to their branches, rebelling against the inevitability of winter's arrival.

The small stadium—home of the Calypso Wildcats—was filled to capacity. Red coats and jackets predominated on the home side, while blue blazed across the field where the visiting Tannersville Tigers had assembled. Throughout the bleachers, steaming thermoses warded off the chill, and spectators clapped their gloved hands together, their breaths hovering in wispy clouds in front of their lips.

The football field was still lush and green, the chalk lines fresh and unmarred under the bright lights. Whooping at the top of their lungs, the Wildcats broke out of the dressing room under the stadium and ran onto the field. They held their helmets aloft, smelling another victory to add to a long string of wins.

Andrew Sinclair led the team onto the field and then crossed to the center to meet with the captain of the opposing team. The two players conferred with the referee, shook hands, and turned to run in opposite directions back to the sidelines. Midway, Andy slowed, looked up into the stands, and raised a clenched fist to the sky. Although his mother was seated high in the reserved section, he caught her eye, and she returned his salute of victory.

This pregame salute had become a talisman for Andy, and CHS fans had been quick to pick it up and make it a ritual of sorts. Now three hundred spectators followed suit to Julia's raised fist while the marching band blared out the school's fight song.

Julia still had a hard time grasping how quickly her boys had grown up. Andy was following in the footsteps of a big brother who had broken a bevy of Calypso's records. Sam was playing junior college football now. When he could, he came home to watch Andy's games, but his team was playing out of state this weekend.

Julia loved the energy that flowed through this stadium every Friday night. And she was unabashedly proud to sit here as the mother of the team's star running back.

The fight song ended in an uproar, and when the noise finally died down, a deep voice boomed over the loudspeaker. "Ladies and gentlemen . . ." The voice belonged to Jake Brighton. Julia couldn't help turning and looking up toward the press box. She saw him standing behind the statisticians, microphone in hand, and a little chill went up her spine. She quickly shook off the unwanted feelings and turned her attention to the man beside her.

Jake's voice echoed again across the field. "Welcome to tonight's game between the Tannersville Tigers and the Calypso Wildcats." Again the crowd erupted into thunderous cheers. "Please rise for our national anthem."

Julia pushed the stadium blanket from her knees and stood up. Beside her, James Vincent put one hand over his heart, the other gently, but possessively, on Julia's back. She looked up at him and smiled.

Julia had met Jim at a church picnic six months ago. She and the boys had begun attending a small community church near their house, and one Sunday afternoon, impulsively, Julia had decided to attend a spring picnic the church was sponsoring. Feeling uncomfortable and out of place at first, Julia found herself seated across from a soft-spoken, friendly man. Jim was tall, balding, and very attractive. Julia was drawn at once to his kind spirit. Over fried chicken and potato salad, they struck up a conversation. Julia learned that Jim's wife of sixteen years had left him (and a teenage son and daughter) to marry another man. Almost two years later, he was still reeling from the rejection. Clumsily, he asked Julia for a date—his first since his college days. Attracted to this man, and feeling a kinship with his suffering, Julia accepted.

Jim was kind and intelligent and had a wonderful sense of humor. He had been born and raised in Calypso and had served as city administrator in the town for the past fifteen years. Julia admired Jim's dedication to his career and his obvious devotion to his still heartbroken children.

The two had found solace in their shared sorrows, and Julia had grown comfortable with Jim. They had become somewhat of an "item" around town, and though the term "going steady" seemed a bit juvenile to Julia, she supposed that they were.

Now Jim cupped his hands and shouted across the stadium as the game began. "Go Wildcats!"

Calypso won the toss and the crowd stayed on its feet for the kickoff. The Wildcats received and ran the ball back to the forty-yard line. When the two teams squared off at the line of scrimmage, Andy carried the ball for a touchdown in the first play of the game.

Julia shot out of her seat and jumped up and down, cheering, her cheeks flushed from excitement and the cold. By the end of the half, Calypso was ahead twenty to seven, and by night's end, they had walked away with the win and a new rushing record for Andy Sinclair.

Though the temperature had dropped below thirty, no one seemed in a hurry to leave the stadium. Parents and students huddled together for warmth in clusters about the bleachers, rehashing each touchdown, play by play. Julia received enthusiastic congratulations for Andy's game, and she vicariously basked in his glory.

When she and Jim finally made their way across the parking lot, it was almost ten thirty. Jim had picked Julia up, and since he lived only six blocks from the high school, they had driven back to his house to park the car. Now they walked briskly arm in arm with stadium blankets around their shoulders, trying to generate some warmth.

"Man, it's freezing!" Jim's words came out in little puffs of steam.

"I know, but we won! We won!" Julia did a little dance—a silly, girlish hopscotch that set them both laughing.

Suddenly Jim's expression changed, and he looked down at her with serious, unsmiling eyes. He took her by the shoulders and, turning her to face him, kissed her full on the lips. "I love you, Julia Sinclair," he said, his usually calm voice fierce with passion. "Do you know that, Julia? I love you."

Julia's heart began to beat rapidly in her chest. It was the first time he had ever spoken those words to her. *Oh, Jim,* she thought, *I'm not sure I'm ready for this*. He kissed her again, gently this time, and stood back, forcing Julia to look into his eyes.

Not knowing how to respond, she just smiled, then impulsively planted another light kiss on his lips. But she couldn't will a declaration of love to form on her lips. She liked Jim—a lot. Maybe she did love him. If so, why did she feel confused?

Had she questioned her love for Martin this way? Even with Jake and all the obstacles of their friendship—when it came to a question of love, there had never been a doubt. Had there?

Since the night Jake had told her goodbye, Julia had prayed—prayed fervently, daily—that God would send her someone. Someone to share conversations the way Jake had. Someone to make her feel as cherished and special as he had. Someone she admired as much as she admired Jake Brighton.

Then Jim had come into her life. In many ways, he was all of those things. He was special, and Julia knew that she was the envy of many women because she "had" Jim. She couldn't have asked for anyone more solicitous toward her sons. She couldn't have asked for anyone with more integrity, or who was more respected in the community.

Her mind churned with questions. Why couldn't she seem to give her heart fully to Jim the way he so obviously had lost his to her? Why couldn't she put the past behind her and embrace the gift of this man's friendship? Why couldn't she put the ghost of Martin, and the living specter of her relationship with Jake Brighton out of her mind? They were both dead to her. They were in her past, and she so desperately wanted to live for today. *Please, Lord, help me. I'm so confused. If this man is a gift from you . . . if this is your will for me, I want to be in it. Show me, Lord. Please, show me. I need to hear from you.*

They walked along the sidewalk toward Jim's house, hand in hand, perfectly in step with each other. Only their boots, pounding out a soft rhythm on the pavement, broke the silence of the chill evening.

But Julia's thoughts spun out of control, a tumultuous irony against the steady rhythm of their footsteps. *He loves me,* she told herself over and over. What more do I want? Julia wondered if she could grow to love Jim with the deep love she remembered from her marriage. Maybe her memory deceived her, and it had taken time to grow into love with Martin—and with Jake. Maybe she just didn't remember.

Jim, in his sweet, quiet way, sensed that she was troubled. "Julia, what's wrong? . . . I'm sorry if I took things too fast back there." He motioned to the sidewalk behind them, as though it were the scene of a crime.

"No, Jim. It's not that." It was a lie, really, but she couldn't bear to hurt him for something of which he was innocent. "I'm just not myself tonight. I'm sorry."

They came to his driveway, and he invited her in for a cup of hot chocolate.

"I'm sorry, Jim. It's awfully late. Would you mind if I beg off tonight? I'd just like to get home."

"Sure." There was disappointment in his voice, but he opened her door for her and went around to start the car. They sat in silence waiting for the car to warm up, but after five minutes, instead of backing out of the driveway, Jim reached into his pocket and took out a small square box. He fumblingly opened the lid and dropped the contents into his palm. Before Julia quite realized what was happening, he reached across the console for her left hand, and pulling her glove off, he slid an exquisite diamond ring onto her finger. It fit perfectly.

His speech was clearly rehearsed, but she knew it came from his heart. "Julia, you have given me so much joy in these past months. I thank God every day for putting you in my life. You have given my life meaning again, and I love you with all my heart. Julia, I don't want to have to take you home ever again. I want our home to be together. I want you to be my wife."

Julia looked down at her hand. The ring's brilliance was magnified through the tears that spilled onto her cheeks.

"Oh, Jim . . . Jim . . ."

16

The morning Ellen died was the kind of day she would have declared perfect. The September sun was tempered by wisps of clouds, and the air was crisp with a foretaste of autumn.

The piercing jangle of the telephone roused Jake from a dreamless sleep. He looked at the clock. Five-thirty A.M. He knew even before he was fully awake that Ellen was gone. He had stayed with her until midnight the night before, listening to her rattled breathing . . . wishing that he could take her next breath for her. Her skin was gray and clammy, and she gasped for air with a strength she hadn't possessed in years. Jake watched her, exhausted with the waiting, until finally the nurses had sent him home, promising to call him if anything changed.

Strange. Tomorrow would have been her birthday. He'd heard that people often held on until a birthday or anniversary. But, of course, Ellen had no awareness of time passing, and she had not been able to make it one more day. The fifty-sixth anniversary of her birth would have to pass without her.

More than three years had passed since Jake had made peace with himself and with God. While the sense of rightness he felt about his renewed commitment to Ellen pervaded everything, still, it hadn't been easy.

In the past year there had been one crisis after another. Ellen caught a virus that left her weak and susceptible to every bug that went around. She ended up with pneumonia, and though she finally pulled through, her lungs were scarred and weakened. In the end, it was pneumonia that came back—this time to claim her.

Mercifully, in the years since Jake had said goodbye to Julia, Ellen had taken on a new, quiet countenance. Jake felt almost as if he had been given a gift . . . a reward for the sacrifices he had made. Yet he knew he had sacrificed nothing in letting Julia go. He couldn't sacrifice what wasn't his. Still, he was grateful for Ellen's peace. It was a thing they could share, a thing they had in common.

When she became bedfast—unable to walk, or feed herself, or even roll over in bed—Jake knew that the end couldn't be far away. He had felt a sort of panic at losing her. This solitary life of being Ellen's husband was all that he knew. He wasn't sure he would know how to live any other way. What was normal, anyway? The normal he could remember from the past was full of teenagers, ball games, parties, boisterous card games, and a pretty wife always at his side. He hadn't had a chance to learn how to live alone— even alone with Ellen. They had been running the treadmill that Alzheimer's had forced them onto for so long. His family nest had been empty for such a long time, and today he would begin to learn how to live in its loneliness.

⸎

Jake arrived at the funeral home early the next morning. It had not occurred to him that walking through the doors of that building meant seeing Ellen. Recorded organ music drifted through the open doors of the sanctuary and drew Jake into the quiet room.

When he saw her lying in the front of the room amid a profusion of flowers, he caught his breath and reached for the back of the pew bench. He half stumbled down the aisle and stood trembling in front of the simple coffin.

She looked almost angelic. Gone were the lines that had creased her forehead. The eyes that in her last years had reflected a haunting confusion, were now peacefully closed. It was freeing for Jake to see Ellen this way. His breathing became more even; his heart ceased its wild pounding. He was overcome with the sense that the ethereal form that lay before him was not Ellen. People at funerals always said the deceased looked as if they were merely sleeping. And though Ellen looked beautiful and at peace, in no way did she look alive to Jake. Her beauty in death was fragile and pearlescent, like that of a seashell. It struck Jake that indeed a shell was what lay before him. The Ellen that Jake Brighton cherished had broken the shard that had long imprisoned her and had flown away home.

Jake slowly looked heavenward and whispered without guilt, "Thank you."

The funeral was a blur of familiar faces, warm with sympathy, but full of relief also. In the front row of the sanctuary Jana and Brant, along with their spouses, sat on either side of Jake. Howard and MaryEllen flanked Kyle, leaning on him for support. They were in their eighties now, stooped and frail, but mentally sharp as ever and strong in spirit.

The past years had aged them both. But, in a way, this day was almost a celebration for them. For all who had loved Ellen and beheld her suffering, this day gave cause for quiet rejoicing.

Jake held Jana's hand tightly, and his mind began to fill with memories of Ellen as she had been before the ogre called Alzheimer's had come into their lives. For the first time in almost a decade, the memories came easily, and they comforted him.

He could see her sitting across from him at the China Garden, laughing and lovely. He saw the tiny apartment in Oscar and Hattie's attic as clearly as if he sat there now. He walked the fields of Ellen's childhood farm again as they said goodbye to their first baby. Perhaps Ellen was holding little Catherine in her arms at this very moment. The thought filled him with joy.

He recalled not the milestones in their life together, but the little things. Impromptu picnics in the backyard when the children were small. Cheering them on at ball games. And the brief time they'd had together after the children were grown—quiet evenings by the fireplace, reading together, making love.

Jake's reverie was broken by the clear, sweet voices of Ellen's nieces. They sang a hymn that Ellen had loved because of the poignant story behind it. The author had penned the lyrics in the nineteenth century after receiving the tragic news that his four beloved daughters had been lost at sea. The melody rose and soared like a living thing through the rafters of the sanctuary.

> When peace like a river attendeth my way,
> When sorrows like sea billows roll;
> Whatever my lot, Thou hast taught me to say,
> It is well, it is well with my soul.

Unexpectedly, Jake's throat swelled and tears rolled unbidden down his cheeks. He thought he had shed all his tears, but the song moved him powerfully.

For so many months, so many endless years, he had been asked to travel a hard and bitter road. But this day he had come to the end of that path, and he could turn and look back from a new, high place. He saw each fork and each rocky incline with clarity, and he knew that his journey had been honorable and not without reason. He could say with conviction, "It is well with my soul."

Epilogue

Jake came in from the backyard to fix himself a glass of tea. It was July, and the air conditioning was on in the house, so he closed the door on the laughter behind him. The quiet of the empty house enveloped him, and he found himself reflective in the sudden silence.

He filled a tall glass with ice from the freezer and poured tea from a huge Mason jar that sat in a pool of sunshine on the floor in the conservatory. Jake smiled as he thought of his wife's insistence that her tea be brewed in the sun. The jar had sat in this spot all summer long—filled some days with raspberry tea, others with lemon—until a ring had formed on the dark oak floor. Once, the stain might have bothered him, marring the otherwise flawless wood. But now it was one of the things that marked this house as theirs—his and the woman he loved. What joy she had brought back to this house on Oaklawn!

There were long months of bitter loneliness after Ellen's death—and yes, bitter years before that. Moments when Jake wasn't sure he could go on another day. When he sought God and felt utterly forsaken. When he screamed "Why?" to the heavens, they were utterly bereft of an answer, only echoing back his own tormented cries . . . *Why? Why? Why?*

In the years after he'd said goodbye to Julia, he had seen her a few times from a distance. But he made no attempt to contact her. It still sickened him when he thought how dangerously close he had come to pulling her into his trespass. In truth, though he knew he had been forgiven, a trace of guilt still lingered for the sin that had almost entrapped him. Strange that temptation could be disguised in a package filled with warmth, caring, and yes, beauty.

And, too, the new purity of his love for Julia—now a chaste love—had kept him from barging back into her life. He wanted in no way to be a source of confusion or a stumbling block to her as she made a new life for herself apart from him.

He had heard through the school grapevine that "Sam and Andy's mom" was dating the city administrator. It still hurt him to think of her happy with someone else. He had to keep reminding himself that Julia was a closed chapter in his life. He could not allow himself to think of reopening the wounds that his sin had inflicted on her—on both of them, really. He had overstepped sacred boundaries, and in doing so, he felt he had lost the right to ever again be a source of happiness to Julia. Through the years, his own wounds had healed over. But there were scars remaining—deep scars that would always be a reminder of his mistakes. He considered himself whole, though, and forgiven; and on another level—a more selfless, honorable plane—he was glad for the news about Julia. He hoped she was finding happiness in her life.

Then, out of the ashes of his grief, when he least expected it, Julia came back into his life. A gift. He smiled at the memory.

He had been at the library—there because he could escape the deafening silence of his house for a different sort of quiet. He was browsing the shelves of biographies, and suddenly she stood beside him.

"Jake. I thought it was you," she had whispered.

"Julia." He had barely been able to speak. He had forgotten how beautiful her voice was. He had not heard that lovely voice for almost five years. Even in a whisper, it stirred him as it always had. Boldly, he asked her if she could go for coffee with him. Was she free? . . . the meaning in his question clear.

They ordered cappuccino in a small cafe across the street from the library. The restaurant was empty, and as they lingered over the warm cups, the years fell away.

"I'm so sorry about Ellen, Jake."

"It seems such a long time ago, Julia. Over a year now; but of course, it was a long time coming. I'm sure you won't judge me if I say it was a blessing."

"No. I understand. Are you doing okay?"

"I've . . . I've been lonely. But I'm all right." He had forgotten how honest he could be with her . . . how comfortable she made him feel. "What about you?"

"Things are good. Different though," she sighed. "Time is going by too fast. The boys are both in college now."

Jake shook his head. "That doesn't seem possible."

"It was hard to send my baby off to school. I thought it was just something people said to make conversation—but kids really do grow up before you know it. I don't know where the time has gone." She shook her head, bewildered. Then she asked brightly, "How are your kids, Jake?"

"Good. Mark and Jana gave me my first grandchild two months ago." He smiled broadly, elated to be sharing this news with her. "She's the world's cutest baby, if I do say so myself."

Julia laughed. "Oh, Jake. That's wonderful! Well, congratulations, Grandpa."

Her laughter brought the memories tumbling back into his mind. How he had missed her. She was beautiful as ever . . . a few more lines creasing her forehead, the honey gold hair a shade darker than before. But as Jake watched her face, she became familiar to his eyes again, to his heart— evoking the things that had made him cherish her so.

"I heard you might be getting married?" It was a bold question, asked tentatively—but Jake had to be certain of their freedom this time.

Julia smiled and shook her head. Her voice was teasing. "Boy, there are no secrets in a small town, are there?" She turned serious. "No, Jake. I was dating—oh, how I hate that word . . ." She rolled her eyes and went on. "I was dating Jim Vincent for . . . well, for quite a while. I guess the rumors got out. He did ask me to marry him, but . . . we're not seeing each other anymore."

"Oh. I'm sorry." Jake couldn't tell if sympathy was in order.

She shrugged. "Don't be sorry. It was my decision. Jim is a wonderful man—salt of the earth. But . . . well, I wasn't in love"—she paused almost imperceptibly—"with him." She dropped her head, suddenly embarrassed by the implication of the pause. "It . . . it didn't seem fair to Jim. I'm afraid I made him wait far too long for an answer." She looked up at Jake. A sadness crept into her eyes, and Jake guessed that it had grieved Julia to hurt Jim by refusing his proposal and eventually breaking off their relationship.

Impulsively, he reached across the table and put his hand over hers. A gesture of warmth, nothing more. But his voice was thick with emotion. "It's great to see you, Julia."

She smiled up at him, joy written on her face.

They talked late into the night, sharing the trials of the years gone by and the joys of the present. And as they spoke, he realized that the love they had once felt for each other had been rekindled—purified now in the fires of obedience and forgiveness.

When he drove her home, and they stood on the porch at her front door, he took her in his arms and pulled her to himself. And he knew it was right. With a full heart, he kissed her over and over. Gently on the forehead, the chin . . . more urgently on the lips. They stood together and cried in each other's arms, not needing to explain their tears. Each knowing they were shed for all the sadness gone before—and for all the joy yet to come.

The gift of liberty was now theirs for the taking. The seed of friendship, the kernel of passion that had been of propriety denied before, now unfolded and blossomed into a thing of beauty. At last they were free to declare their love, to celebrate their passion for each other.

⊗

They had married in the spring. The ceremony was in the big backyard on Oaklawn with all their children gathered around them. And now Julia graced this home with her joyful spirit. He had known immeasurable blessings these past months.

Jake replaced the lid on the jar of tea and started back through the kitchen. He glanced out the tall window that looked out over the backyard. The lacy filigree of the curtains diffused the light, giving a surreal, dreamlike quality to the scene beyond. Spellbound, he gazed at the tableau before him.

Mark and Jana stood arm in arm at the edge of the lawn.

Brant and a very pregnant Cynthia, and Kyle and Lisa, Kyle's bride of two weeks, were sprawled comfortably on the grass. Beside them, Sam and Andy—young men now—smiled as they watched their mother.

Julia stood in the middle of the lawn, barefoot and radiant in a pink summer dress. A squealing, sun-browned toddler romped at her feet as the lawn sprinkler sent a spray of glittering water high into the air above them. The icy droplets hit their target and fresh peals of happy laughter floated on the summer air into the kitchen where Jake stood.

Mark and Jana's little Ellen Marie was a tiny ray of hope, a budding promise of this family's blessing for the future. She had Ellen's dark curls and blue-gray eyes. And when she smiled, Jake saw a reflection of Ellen's beautiful face. Such a sweet memorial to her namesake.

Everything that was precious to him was embodied in the scene before him. His family was bound together with an everlasting cord of love and commitment and faith.

An array of emotions washed over him—hope . . . joy . . . the most transcending peace he had ever known. His throat swelled, and he sent a prayer of profound gratitude heavenward.

Jake opened the door and stepped out into the yard. Across the wide expanse of grass came the joyful cries of a curly-haired little girl. She ran toward him on pudgy legs, her silvery voice calling, "Grandpa! Grandpa!"